and KILL ONCE MORE

AL FRAY

A GRAPHIC MYSTERY

AND KILL ONCE MORE

One

I LAY on the Santa Monica strand and watched lazy fall breakers pile in. Each long slow wave rolled shoreward, mounting higher and higher until at last the crest toppled over and crashed toward me in a broad curtain of white foam, then spent itself on the sand and washed silently back into the surf. Hungry sandpipers followed the backwash, their long needle-like beaks darting into the wet sand in search of an early snack. A squadron of gulls wheeled overhead and morning sunlight gave a sparkle to the blue Pacific, a glitter which, for me at least, has never lost its attraction. I stood up, stretched, weighed the empty feeling in my stomach against the lure of salt water and decided on another dip before breakfast.

The water had just enough snap to feel right. I splashed through the surf, knifed into a seven foot wall of white and came up on the other side. Working easily out a hundred yards, I rolled over and lay on the swells, my thoughts on the beach and how things were and how they might go on being for quite a while. Summer had gone the way of a lot of other summers; now it was October. Next month the inn at Death Valley would open and I'd hold forth as combination lifeguard and swimming instructor for the winter season, then knock off for another vacation and when warm weather brought the multitude down to the ocean there would be a job for Marty Bowman.

A nice life—until there comes a day when you begin to wonder if thirty-one isn't getting a little old for a beach boy and wouldn't it be smart to look around for something a bit more permanent. But thinking back over some of the other times I'd tried to make the break brought a smile to my face. There was that fall I took a job punching rivets in an aircraft plant. Not too hard, a nice clean, respectable spot but somewhere along the second week I figured out that at the rate of one every ten seconds I was forty million rivets from retirement and that's just too damn many rivets. I asked for my time and caught on with a plunge down in Palm Springs for the rest of the winter.

And there have been other times, other jobs I've taken and some I tried for without success but somehow I always wind up wearing swimming trunks, dark glasses, and a towel over my shoulders. Maybe the real reason I can't get interested in running a drill press is that in the back of my mind there's a picture of the enterprise I hope to launch some day. A small but classy pool well located on the fringes of Beverly Hills, perhaps, and set up to skim off some of the easy dough spilling out of pockets in that area. Swimming lessons for small fry during the day and party rental at night—work I could really enjoy and at the same time lay away a buck or so, and. . . .

Vaguely I was aware that the pounding of the surf had increased and the swells had carried me toward the beach. I turned and stroked along ahead of a rising crest, caught it breaking, and rode all the way in. When it petered out under me and dribbled back toward the sea I jogged up onto the dry sand, caught up my towel and went toward my small beach cottage. Before I opened the door I heard the phone ringing. I went inside, crossed the narrow hallway, dropped the towel on the carpet, stepped on it and picked up the phone.

"Marty Bowman," I said.

"Marty? Boreland Gregory." He let that soak in for a second, then said, "Marty, I have an assignment for you. A client is with me now, a young lady who seems to have a rather unusual problem. It's your type of thing and I'd like you to handle it."

I stood there, the phone in my hand and salt water dripping onto the towel. There couldn't be any mistake. Boreland Gregory was my brother's boss and the few times Gregory had dialed my number it was in an effort to locate Fred. Now Gregory was calling me. He had used my first name slowly and deliberately. Twice.

"Hold on," I said. "I just came up from the beach and I'd better dry off."

But I wasn't worried about a few drops of water. I needed time to square this one away. Somebody was obviously right at Gregory's elbow. He couldn't say what he wanted to say, couldn't make any explanations. Over the wire I heard his voice again, low this time as though he'd turned away. "How's that for service, Miss Weston? Our man Bowman just came out of the water."

If the Miss Weston in his office answered I didn't hear her but I was getting a line on things. Gregory had a Bowman on his staff all right but it wasn't me. Fred has been an ace investigator with the Gregory Agency for a dozen years and once tried to grease the chute there for me. He arranged an interview and I went down, but the deal didn't jell. We'd gotten along fine until Boreland Gregory tilted back in his heavy oak chair, fixed a shrewd eye on my face and asked how he could be sure, after investing his time and money to train me for his work, that it wouldn't all go slipping down the drain when summer came and the beaches called. I didn't try to kid him. I said he couldn't be sure at all and right about then he lost interest in adding Marty Bowman to his payroll.

Two years ago, that was, but now things had suddenly changed. Now Gregory was making a noise like a man who was over the barrel. It was obvious he needed somebody who owned more than one pair of trunks, you might say, and I thought about the month I had to kill before the inn opened and decided against giving him the kiss-off.

"You're getting through to me," I said softly. "What can you tell me over the phone? What do we do about—"

"Fine," he cut in. "We'll take care of the odds and ends when you get here. Just pack a bag and hurry down to the office. Miss Weston is due at a house party on the desert, Marty, but she's a little worried. Needs help on a couple of matters. You're going as a guest, so put some swimming trunks into a suitcase and be on your way. You might take about what you'd want for a nice weekend in a first class resort, but don't forget those trunks. Got that?"

"The swimming trunks," I echoed softly. "Yes, I think I get the picture, Mr. Gregory. I'll be there as soon as possible—about twenty minutes. Anything else?"

"She'll wait for you, Marty. Make it fast."

The phone clicked and I cradled it, then hit for the shower. Hot water splashed across my shoulders and washed away the salt while I did a mental retake on the fragment of a picture Boreland Gregory had given me, and five minutes later I climbed into my four-year-old coupe, whipped over onto Wilshire Boulevard and headed toward Hollywood. Gregory's agency is on the second floor in a building just off the celebrated corner, so I found a parking spot on Vine and walked back.

Before I got to the entrance a familiar voice greeted me. "Hi, kid. Or should I call you lucky?"

I turned toward the curb and saw my brother Fred leaning against a light blue Cadillac with gleaming wire wheels. "Delayed action?" I asked. "Two years ago I hit fat boy for a job and today it comes through. You sure I'm lucky?"

Fred gave me an envious grin. "There isn't much doubt about that," he said. He turned to admire the

Cad again and nodded his appreciation, then touched a respectful toe to a spotless white sidewall. "Your carriage, m'lord. And wait till you see the lady in waiting. Enough to make me wish I'd put more time on the beach and less chasing after some jerk's erring spouse. Now let's get inside before the boss has a litter of pups on the office floor. He's been hopping from one foot to the other ever since he phoned you." I followed my brother into the narrow hall and started up the stairway but he stopped me.

"Let's see your wallet, kid."

I handed it over and watched him cram a sheaf of twenties into it. Then he made another small transfer and passed it back. Those little odds and ends that Gregory had mentioned were now taken care of.

"Three hundred, Marty. Pay all the tabs and keep account. Strictly a smooth operation; he'll nick her for the expenses later, but don't let her shell it out any place along the line. Catch?"

"Sure, but—"

"No time for a bull session, kid. Now take this and keep it out of sight. A prop, see?" Fred carefully handed over his stubby .38. "If she happens to see it, fine. Anybody else, not good. You've got no license. Now toss me the keys to your hack and I'll run it back out to the beach for you."

I gave him the keys, then took another peek into the wallet. "Take Martha and Tim," I called after Fred. "There's a new surfboard in the garage if Tim wants to try those breakers again." Fred waved his thanks and I climbed the stairs to Gregory's office.

Seeing him again brought me back to the business at hand and a wave of doubts began to roll in. In one corner of my mind was the nagging thought that all was not kosher along Vine Street this fine morning. It didn't quite fit, this quick and easy entrance of Marty Bowman into the glamorous role of the shamus. Boreland Gregory had spent a lot of years building his name in this town and he was nobody's chump. He was getting bald, had a figure like a couple of bags of barley, flat feet, cash register eyes, and other dubious assets that added up to nothing impressive on the physical side, but his mind was as sharp as a well-honed razor. From his swiveled throne in the bay window of a lush Hollywood office he ran one of the most profitable detective agencies in town and was far too smart a business man to risk a fine reputation in the hands of an untried operator. Yet from where I stood it looked like he was doing just that. I was still asking myself why.

The receptionist ushered me through the heavy door and the situation didn't improve. Gregory waddled out from behind six feet of battered oak desk, made hasty introductions, pointed out that time was fleeting, said we'd have a good sixty miles to discuss things and urged the pair of us to be on our way. I shot a hard look his way. It didn't seem to me that B.G. was very worried over the girl's problem, whatever it was, and he should have been because another of his specialties is extracting the long green from the patrons and at his prices he could afford to show a little concern. It would have been no more than good business.

When I turned back his Miss Weston was giving me the slow top-to-bottom and I tossed it back at her. She was blonde and tan and would have been a knockout anyplace. Not too tall, a refreshing change from the amazons some people turn out these days and one quick look told you she was as feminine as a negligee. You didn't have to be an expert on women's apparel to guess that the blue gabardine suit had come from an exclusive shop and her white, high-heeled shoes had a simple elegance associated with good taste and a healthy bank balance. Without being too obvious I glanced down long enough to assure myself that the part of her between those shoes and the hem line was as fine a bit of leg as you'll find on any beach. I thought about that racy Caddy standing against the curb outside, then picked up my bag and nodded toward the door. I had this pigeon pegged.

These stacked jobs with a few bucks behind them run pretty much to form. They come down to the beach wearing that go-to-hell look and not much more and never look to right or left, but every guy within seeing distance is straining his eyes and pawing the sand—and well they know it. I've picked up a few things besides splinters, though, while sunning myself in those life-guard towers and I figured to get along with this cutie.

We went through the office and started down the narrow stairway and glancing back I saw Boreland Gregory smiling after us. His face wore the expression of a used-car salesman who has just unloaded the junkiest heap on the lot and it worried me a little.

At the bottom of the steps the blonde turned back toward me to make a casual remark about the weather and it told me something else about her. You didn't have to beat her to the door. She knew the trick of hesitating long enough to give a man time to reach around her and turn the knob. No obvious stepping aside to wait, no pushing on through by herself—just a lady letting you be the gentleman. When we walked out to the curb I swung the car door and installed her on the side next to the walk, then tossed my scuffed gladstone into the back, next to a pair of matched traveling cases worth about ninety bucks a print, and slid in behind the wheel.

Over Cahuenga Pass we got it down to Kate and Marty and worked in a few background details but the blonde gave the problem at hand a wide berth. Vague generalities and the bland statement that it would be easier to show me when we arrived. Maybe I shouldn't have worried about it, either. Good duty this. I should have been content to roll her expensive wagon over the concrete and let small matters take care of themselves but somehow I didn't like the feel of things. We turned right onto the Canyon Highway, the tires making a soothing hum on the pavement. Dry air hung motionless over stunted desert growth and dusty tumbleweeds shook themselves at our passing, bumped lazily along in our wake for a few yards, and subsided in the peace of the morning. Tiny heat waves shimmered over rocks and sand and in the distance a range of ragged hills swept upward and caught purple tints from a climbing sun.

I pushed the lighter into contact, and tried to figure who was kidding who, and why. When the lighter clicked back I offered smokes, then held the glowing tip for Miss Weston. Her thank you was a smile backed by those cool blue eyes and then she settled back again to watch the scenery slip past. She was as relaxed as a rag doll. She had draped the jacket to her suit over the back of the seat and a stream of air deflected inward by the windwing tugged gently at that long yellow hair and arranged her thin nylon blouse into that rounded effect cover girls strive to achieve. We smoked in silence, the soft purr of two hundred willing horses whisked us effortlessly along, and once again I tried to make something sensible out of the hour that had elapsed since I answered my phone back on the beach.

A house party at a desert hideaway. Bring swimming trunks, there's a pool. Miss Weston has a problem, one which she seems in no hurry to discuss. Well, Marty Bowman wanted to discuss it, and the quicker the better. I devoted another half mile to trying to think of a smooth way of getting her to tear into the facts, then decided on the direct approach.

"Look, Kate, I'm having a wonderful time and the desert is grand this time of year and all that, but you're paying money and you're entitled to service. You won't get it unless I know a lot more than I do now, so let's stop sparring around. Exactly what do you want done up here? What was I hired to do?"

She met my eyes, then looked straight ahead. "First let's be sure we know what you're not expected to do. My hiring a man to go on a house party could look like something—something it definitely isn't. Let's be sure to remember that I called a detective agency and not a gigolo service, shall we?" She blew a cloud of smoke to one side and kept her eyes on the sleek hood out front. I drew on my own smoke and scratched around for an answer, then saw a small café coming into sight at the next bend. I braked the big car with a loss of a couple of miles of rubber, wheeled off onto the gravel parkway, stopped next to a cream and brown Pontiac hard-top, and turned off the ignition.

"Coffee stop, your ladyship," I said shortly. "And while we're getting everyone in his place let's not lose sight of one important fact. You came to us. I wasn't out nosing around for a little Miss Gotrocks." I started to get out of the car but the blonde reached over and caught my arm.

"It isn't like that, Marty. I mean it's just that—"

"You're blonde and beautiful," I cut in, my voice jumping a little. "Your chassis would put you in the front row of the chorus or set you up as a free-lance model if you had to make a living, but this wagon we're sporting around in says you don't need the dough. Which brings us to your point—you're not the type that has to hire boy friends. Now let's see about that coffee, shall we?"

"I'm sorry, Marty. It did sound cheap, I guess."

I looked hard at her and ran my hand over the soft gray leather of the big Cadillac. The idea trying to form itself in my mind for the last half hour finally took shape and this wasn't my day to be coy.

"Kiddo," I said softly, "could this all be a gag? A lot of people with too much money and not enough amusement and one of them says, 'Why doesn't someone bring up a private eye next weekend? We'll give him something to investigate just for laughs. We'll have us a ball.' If that's the way it is, Kate, just say the word. We'll scoot back to San Fernando and pick up a double-billed cap and give 'em a real belly laugh." I watched her face, saw the sudden flush of anger, edged by a hint of fear.

"Of course not, Marty. Mr. Gregory assured me that you'd be specially careful not to let anyone know. You were to go as a friend."

"Then why not keep all the mystery on the other side? Just between friends, what's wrong up here? So far all I've got to go on is that someone called Sandy Engle hasn't been going out much lately, and that there's always a flock of guests."

Kate ran a slow hand over her temple, then let the hand fall to her lap and pluck nervously at the band of her tiny watch.

"Marty, there are really two things at the Engle Ranch that just don't add up. First there's Sandy—Mrs. Engle. I've known her ever so long, since we were children, and she's the type that loves to see and be seen, as the phrase has it, and yet in the two—" She broke off as the screen door of the café slammed. A man and woman came heavily down the wooden steps. I felt Kate stiffen against the leather seat.

"The Pilchers," she whispered. "They'll probably be guests up there this weekend. I've seen them there twice."

They were both big people, though not too many years over thirty. The woman gave us a quick glance, faltered as recogniton came to her, then went on without a word.

She was brown haired and going to hips and might have looked a little less pudgy in something that fit rather than straining the seams of a dress two sizes too small. But it wasn't a cheap dress.

Her husband did a double take when he saw the blonde beside me, then ambled our way. He had a red baseball cap cocked back at a jaunty angle, a toothpick between his thick lips, and a brothers-in-misery sneer on his kisser. He folded his elbows across the chrome window trim on the Cad, shifted his toothpick a little and grinned at the girl.

"Hell of a note, isn't it, Miss Weston?"

"I'm afraid I don't understand, Mr. Pilcher," Kate said evenly. "You said something like that once before, up at the ranch, but really I—"

The brotherly grin turned to a sarcastic look and he backed off from the Cad.

"Hell, I forgot. You're the one that comes up here to smell the sagebrush. 'Scuse me all to hell."

I slid out of the big car and went around just as he was working his fat can behind the wheel of his Pontiac. I pulled the door out of his hand and put a foot along the floor trim.

"Getting a little near-sighted, aren't you neighbor? That was a lady you were talking to." I said it softly and waited. Chubby squinted up at me, his eyes shifting over me as he weighed the possibilities. I didn't think I ought to leave any doubt in his mind. I gathered a handful of shirt, gave it a half twist and hauled him out onto the gravel, then let him straighten up. He stood there blowing hard breaths through his thick lips and I measured him with a watchful eye because there's no point in leaving yourself open for the sucker punch. If he so much as tightened a face muscle I was going to hang one on him. He looked away, turned back, didn't see any change in my eyes, and faced the big Cad.

"Sorry—Miss Weston. I made a mistake," he said.

I watched him wiggle back into his car, fire it up, back around and gun out onto the highway. He headed north and disappeared around a bend as I opened the car door for Kate.

I grinned. "I still want that coffee, Kate."

We found a booth. A tired gent in a white shirt and apron was busy cutting the day's delivery of pies near the front. Kate and I settled, ordered coffee when the man came over, watched him leave, and looked across at each other.

"Thanks, Marty. I'm not sure you should have, but thanks."

"You were going to tell me a couple of things that were out of step up at the ranch," I reminded her. "The first had to do with Sandy Engle." I shook a couple of cigarettes loose and held the pack across the table, then struck a mach from the folder on the ashtray. She puffed quickly and glanced nervously toward the distant waiter.

"Well—it looks like you got the second part first. As guests at the ranch, Pilcher isn't the exception, he's the rule. They all have one thing in common. They resent being there. They give the impression they are forced to come and bullied into making believe they like it."

Two

THE WAITER brought two steaming cups, slid one in front of me, made a production of arranging the other for Kate and went reluctantly back to subdividing his pies. I offered sugar, tipped a half spoon into my own cup and gave it a slow round-and-round.

"That brings us to me, Kate," I said quietly. "I haven't

asked to be invited either—but what about you? You're a guest up there quite often, or so you say." I made it sound like a question. Two blue eyes caught mine and held on, and when she spoke her voice asked for a small measure of confidence.

"Would I hire you to find out something I already know?"

I didn't answer but I remembered a couple of years back a blonde babe pushing thirty, trim and wearing forty dollars worth of bathing suit, came down to the plunge in one of those swank Las Vegas hotel pools. I had the duty and this chick decided to take a few lessons. She started out by sputtering and thrashing the water and in half an hour I had her paddling across the pool. I was feeling real proud of myself until it crossed my mind that she'd learned just a little too fast and it came out later that this was one hell of a way from her first dip. There was something about her being on the 1948 Olympic swimming team and we had a good laugh over it in the bar later that evening. Looking across at Kate, I reminded myself not to bite down too hard on everything she handed out. It might not all be candy.

I sipped hot brown coffee and sifted a few possibilities, then leaned forward and swept salt and pepper shakers, the sugar bowl, ashtray, and napkin holder over to the wall. Except for our cups that cleared the table.

"Let's dive in and get wet all the way, Kate," I said. "You think something is off the beat up at the Engle ranch. Okay, we'll start with what we have and see where it leads us. So far we've agreed that people don't want to go up there but they do go and what's more, they try to make believe they like it. But not you. Right? You're not in the general setup." I brought the sugar bowl back and put it in the center of the table. "That's point one. Now what's different about you? What sets you apart from the other guests?"

She drummed polished fingernails on the shiny table and thought it over. "I really don't know. There doesn't seem to be any place to start."

"Who invites you, George or Sandy?"

"Sandy of course."

"Well, does she know the other people or are they friends of his? I mean did she know them before they came up there?"

Kate's eyes widened and for several seconds she stared at me. When she answered her voice was tense and I could see the glow of excitement rising in her face.

"I can't be sure about Sandy, but I haven't known a single one of them before George and Sandy moved up here. And for several years before she married we ran together quite a bit. They shouldn't all be strangers to me, should they?"

I brought over the salt shaker and put it beside the sugar. "Another small point," I grinned. "Maybe we're going to get a yard or two here. How long have they had this desert hideaway?"

"Almost two years."

"How often do you park your suitcase in their guest room?"

"Actually," she laughed, "Sandy and I don't stand on formal invitations. I drive up whenever I feel in the mood, maybe every six weeks or so, but not on a pre-arranged schedule. They have plenty of guest space and I just phone and say I'll be there."

"And you sometimes find a friend to bring?"

"No. This is the first time—but Sandy was more than glad to have me invite someone."

I reached for the napkin holder. "Then there is this business about Sandy Engle not leaving the old homestead. What about that, Kate?"

"That's the thing that really worries me, Marty. As I said, Sandy and I have been one-two for a lot of years.

We traded school girl secrets in junior high and com-
pared notes on dates when we were in Beverly Hills High
School and all the rest. Same sorority at USC and I was
the maid of honor when she and George went down the
aisle three years ago and if there's anyone in California
that I know especially well it's Sandy Engle. She's a girl
who likes to get around and always has. Yet in the two
years that she and George have had their estate up in
the canyon, she hasn't left the grounds once. Not once
—and I've got to know why."

"You mean that literally. She's never been outside the
fence—if there is a fence, that is."

"There's a fence, and it isn't locked but it might as
well be as far as Sandy is concerned," Kate said grimly.

I set the napkin holder down. "That's good enough for
point three until a better one comes along." I grinned.
"Who shops for the necessities like beer and mink coats
and an occasional loaf of bread?"

Kate ground out her cigarette and searched my face
with a puzzled eye. "You're joking of course." She
smiled thinly. "Sandy has the mink all right, and the
things that go with it, all except one. A mink coat isn't
of much use unless people see it and to see Sandy's fur
you have to drive up to the desert."

"Does she hint that she'd like to break out? What does
she offer as a reason for her exile?"

"Now that I think of it, she doesn't let the subject
come out in the open. She never talks about it or anything, just sits on the nest. Whenever I invite her to my
place in Hollywood she makes some hasty excuse and
turns to a different subject." Kate looked down and her
fingers twisted together nervously. They stopped and she
looked up. "This may sound silly—but her eyes haven't
gotten the word, Marty. She wants to get away. I'm sure
of it. Sure enough to have looked up the Gregory Agency
in the yellow pages of the phone book. She couldn't have

changed, Marty. Not Sandy. Not that much. She's—she's somehow a prisoner, and yet—"

Across the counter the old fellow had finished dividing the pastry and was sliding the pieces into a mirrored display case. I caught his eye long enough to order a couple of more cups of coffee and went back to the chore at hand.

"You wouldn't have gone this far without having come to a conclusion of some kind," I said easily. "Coming to Gregory is costing you money. What have you decided?" She glanced up, then gave me a meaningful look and toyed with the spoon until our coffee refills spilled into the cups. When we were alone again she bit her lip and looked away.

"Some way George is keeping Sandy there. I mean I think he is and—"

"How could he?" I asked quickly.

"I don't quite know. Still—if he isn't, somebody is."

It wasn't much, and I said, "There's a constitutional amendment against that sort of thing. If she's being held against her will we'll get her out."

The blonde flashed me a dim smile that said she wasn't completely sold. I wasn't, either. I let the conversation wither while we went through the second cup of coffee, then dropped a half buck on the table and ushered her out to her expensive collection of chrome and gray leather. One thing for sure, if this was a gag someone had gone to a lot of trouble building it.

We eased out onto the highway and rolled north, the big car logging the miles pleasantly and silently. I went over the facts again and tried to get a foothold—not only on what she'd told me, but the small aura of involuntary information that clung to her and the rest of the setup. The one common denominator was money. Where there's a lot of it, there're usually people eager to get their hands on it. In this case that could get to include me.

And what about Sandy's staying so close to the family circle? I thought about that and a different light fell across it, dim and obscure, yet perhaps touching on possibilities. If she didn't leave, she wouldn't be any place else— maybe she had a reason for staying at the ranch against her will. In short, Sandy Engle could be hiding up in these hills—I tossed a sidelong look at the blonde, wondering if the same thought had occurred to her.

The sun was beginning to make itself felt. I touched a button and rolled the rear windows down into their wells. It didn't help. Then the blonde put a finger on the buttons on her side and rolled all of the windows back up. Tight. Then another button and somewhere a soft motor hummed to life and settled back down to near silence as it attained speed. The car began to cool. I blew a slow breath through rounded lips and shook my head.

"Let's talk about money, Kate," I said. "We peasants choose a new car now and then, something out of what is laughingly called the low price range but they're still listed in the consumers' guides. Also listed there, just to give us something to work for, are the class wagons and I seem to remember that the air-conditioning unit you just turned on is listed as an extra, available at something over six hundred bucks a copy. Now if you and the Engle woman were so buddy-buddy for humpteen years, she must have had a bit of scratch too. Tell me, how was she fixed before she married G.E. and what about him?"

She gave me a cool look and I guessed she was trying to decide whether or not I was being personal so I raised a business-like eyebrow and waited. "Sandy didn't have a tremendous amount of money but I'm sure she didn't have to count the pennies."

"And George?"

"He has a business in L.A. Insurance. The subject hasn't come up, of course, but I gather that he does rather well."

"Wait a second," I said quickly, my foot coming off the gas. "You mean he commutes to L.A. from here. Sixty miles each way every day?"

"No." Kate touched a tongue to her red lips and looked across at me. "He's what is commonly called 'an older man'—that is, he's probably a good twenty years older than Sandy. Maybe fifty-one or two. Naturally he has his affairs in smooth working order and only goes to the office a couple of mornings a week."

"Oh," I said, and tried to give it an understanding tone, but I wasn't convinced. I put the gas back down and the car responded with instant vigor. I thought about some of the insurance agents I know. None of them can make a living in two days a week. Sure, a couple of them are doing all right but they open the office at nine and twelve hours later they're out beating their gums in somebody's parlor. Long hours. And Engle builds a mansion in the hills on part time work? Easy, Marty. There might be something here.

I drove fast and tried to make my mind keep pace with the wheels. I didn't have much to go on, but Engle just might be conducting some business at home that didn't stand to be talked about, and that might explain the unwilling guests. In which case we might all be eventually embarrassed—even Sandy.

When I looked across at the girl I caught her giving me a thoughtful eye. With the windows closed and no breeze whipping through the car her long blonde hair fell almost to her shoulders and she sat against the gray leather with an easy grace you don't run across very often. I wanted to reach over and pat her tan cheek and tell her everything was going to be all right and to stop worrying. But that wouldn't have accomplished much and instead I decided to start a new chain of questions.

The blonde beat me to the punch, "Have you been with the Gregory Agency for quite a while, Marty?"

I let a frown work across my face but the question wasn't exactly unexpected. I'd been thinking of an answer for a good thirty miles.

"Be careful you don't trip over my long white beard," I said, "because Gregory has been handing pay checks to Bowman for almost twelve years. Satisfied?" I finished with a dubious smile, and salved my conscience with the fact that I hadn't told her a direct lie. I hadn't said which Bowman.

"I didn't mean it that way," she laughed, and pinked a little "It's just that you're burned so brown and you—don't exactly look like a detective."

"Two questions—" I grinned—"and I'll answer them both. As you can probably guess the hours are a little irregular. Some of the boys go fishing, some sleep; I pile up beach time. And a detective that looked like a detective couldn't earn enough money to file an income tax report. The good ones look like bookkeepers or salesmen or carpenters."

She touched a tongue to her lips again and a twinkle came into her eye. "I know one that looks like something you see down on Muscle Beach most any Sunday morning."

"You pursue your hobby and I'll keep mine," I said. "This being a working day for me, though, it might be best if we slipped back to things a little closer to the business at hand. I was going to ask some more questions about the guests and our man George Engle. Feel like talking a while?"

As the big Caddy rolled over the highway I listened and tried to slide things into place. The George and Sandy marriage was definitely a going affair. He was older than she—a hell of a lot older—but Kate was sure they were quite the happy couple. Married three years ago, lived in the city for a while, then the sudden shift to the hills and sand. No explanations, just building a desert home in the bleak foothills edging the Mojave. A permanent setup, complete with pool and a dozen guest rooms.

Visits by many friends, both sexes, but of the old gang only Kate was invited. George ran the rest of the guest list. And his wife held down the fort with a vigilance hardly to be expected of a wife so young. Two years and not off of the grounds. Now Kate was worried.

A worried blonde with plenty of scratch in her handbag. Enough to roll her expensive hack down to the best agency in Hollywood and part with one of Boreland Gregory's king-size retainers just to see what was keeping her little friend on the nest.

A few more miles and Kate called a turn. We wheeled left off of the highway and onto a narrow tarred road. We began to gain a little altitude. Tar pavement gave way to gravel but it was carefully graded and fairly wide. It wound into the opening of a canyon and started up at an even steeper angle. Hairpin turns and switchbacks. Then we saw it.

Almost on the ridge but not quite—low enough to let the hill break the wind. Rambling in the Southern California mode, and even from below you could see that it was something special in the way of desert mansions. It came in and out of sight as we rounded tight turns and changed direction, and when I pulled the Cad hard to the left and circled an embankment we rolled onto the concrete parking strip in front of a six-car garage. The cream and brown Pontiac belonging to Pilcher stood at one end of the apron and a black Lincoln was beside it. I eased the Cad to a stop, went around to the other side and held the door for Kate. For once I wasn't looking at her.

"Nice layout, isn't it?" She smiled.

I didn't answer. Hers was the understatement of the morning and I couldn't improve on it. Bright new concrete block had been painted a soft desert blue and while the area outlying from the block fence was brown and parched, inside everything was green and rich with life. A park. An estate which, had it not been so obviously new, might have been a holdover from the years when fabulously wealthy movie stars, in those lush years before heavy income tax, built great showplaces above Beverly Hills.

I blew a slow breath and reached for the bags, but a Philippino was hurrying toward us. I straightened again and had one more look at the Engle resort.

For a man who worked only a couple of mornings a week George Engle was doing right well.

Three

BY MID-AFTERNOON I was beginning to adjust to life as the other half lives it. I stroked slowly toward the shallow end of twenty thousand dollars worth of swimming pool and reflected on the tidy little estate that Engle had managed to afford on a two-day working week. The main building was a huge U-shaped, inn-like structure which provided a fine windbreak for one side and both ends of the plunge. Beyond the center segment the hill rose sharply for a short distance and atop the crest an enormous storage tank gathered water pumped in from a dozen distant hot springs. A wide expanse of grass separated the house from the pool on those sides but to the south a thick growth of Italian cypress ran close to the concrete fringe of the plunge and blocked desert winds which would blow with considerable vigor at certain seasons. Leading through the cypress, a flagstone walk wound through heavy shrubbry and down the slope toward the service building that housed the valve for the pool.

Everything inside the fence was green and carefully

tended, a marked relief from the parched, brown desert surrounding us, and standing on the lower edge of the estate you could look past the barren land and into a green valley to which irrigation had brought a new value. But the center of interest which completely dominated the estate was George Engle's swimming pool. Oval, roughly thirty by fifty and a full fifteen feet at the deep end, she was a far cry from the pint capacity leaf-catchers scattered around L.A. Like I said, I've dreamed of operating one on a commercial basis and as a prospective customer I've shopped around a little as to cost and upkeep of these things and there is a hell of a lot more to it than digging a hole, cementing the sides, and filling it from the garden hose.

True, you have to dig a hole. It costs money—important money if you have any amount of rock formation running under your land, and it's also true that you cement the walls and bottom of the thing. But a bit of pencil work coupled with a few facts you picked up in high school physics will tell you that there's a lot of weight on the floor of that pool. To be exact there's just over sixty-two pounds per square foot for every foot of depth—over nine hundred pounds pushing downward on each square foot at the deep end of Engle's pool. That means steel reinforcement and plenty of it, along with several inches of concrete. Money—money—money.

Then there is a drainage system. The common way is to fill the pool once and use that water continuously, adding only enough to take care of evaporation loss. This requires an expensive filter system, pumps, and man hours, but even so it beats changing water. Then there is heat. Let's not kid about it—water standing around gets cold, even in Southern California, in the winter. Or every night, for that matter, and while some of us might like it cool enough to be invigorating the guests you invite won't go for it and that means heat. An added expense, but there it is. You'll have to do something about keeping down the algae and every so often you'll have to apply a coating to the entire surface. Time and materials and more cash down the drain.

Now add the cleaning, and it's a major headache. Dust blowing across the street keeps right on going and eventually whisks off the far side but when those tiny particles hit the water in your pool, they stay. The dirt settles to the bottom in a thin brown film and about every other day you have to peel off and get in for some wet work or push with the long pole from the edge. The gadget that cleans your pool isn't too different from the vacuum sweeper in principle—it sucks up water and dirt from the bottom, runs it through the filter and returns it to the plunge—but you'll get a lot of exercise on the handle of it just the same.

That's the usual private plunge setup and like I say it's expensive, but basking in the warmth of George Engle's pool I watched lazy vapors drift upward from the storage tank on the hill and thought about how different this one was. Not that the idea is original. It isn't; there are several like it scattered around wherever you find natural hot springs. For this kind of layout you capture half a dozen warm springs, pump the water up to a big reservoir, buy enough flat land down below to engage in extensive irrigation operations, and establish the cycle. Fill the swimming pool early, paddle around in the warm water all day, and at night you drain the now cool water into a lower tank for the crops below, hose down the sides and bottom, and fill the clean pool with fresh warm water from the storage above. Each day sees newly pumped warm water in the pool and by the time it cools you are through with it and can refill again.

And all you need is a few hundred thousand dollars to find the hot springs and buy the land and lay the pipe and provide pumps, tanks, plunge, and a ranch in the valley. Just a little pin money you scrape together a couple of days a week.

I was still trying to nail these scattered facts into some sort of pattern when I heard a splash at the deep end. Kate Weston bobbed up near the center and swam toward me with strong smooth strokes. When she came up to me she flashed a wet smile and I paddled along beside her for a way. We made two lazy laps of Engle's triumph in tile and stainless steel fittings, then climbed out near a couple of light green patio pads near the shallow end and spread out to sun ourselves.

Kate glanced toward the assorted people sprawled over deck furniture on the far side and said softly, "Anything new, Marty?"

I grinned at her. "It gets worse."

"You've found out something?"

"I've found out nothing," I admitted, "or very little. You sure there's something wrong?"

Kate slipped her white bathing cap off and let long blonde hair tumble down to the pad. I ran an appreciative eye over her trim brown lines and expensive bathing suit, then came back to catch two blue eyes looking mildly across at me.

"If there isn't, there's something wrong about me."

"That could be."

A thin smile played along her eyes. "And what have we decided about the rest of the customers, Marty?"

I grinned. "Let's not be bitter. You can learn a lot about people around the water. Like your friend Pilcher over there. This morning he appeared to be a fat and mouthy gent with nothing to back it up. The picture hasn't changed. A while ago he dove in beside me and started swimming away with that 'wanna race' look in his face. He has to impress people. You can see him on the beach any afternoon, or several like him. They spread their over-stuffed skins on the sand and rest for ten minutes. Then some kid comes along and fat boy has to dive into the surf and make like a teen-ager. When he climbs out panting like an overworked steam engine he tries to muffle the sound of his breath. Ninety per cent of the time his belly overflows his trunks, but let some cute chick waltz by and our pudgy friend will suck that tummy up into a chest that would scare a gorilla, flex his muscles, and try to hold it until she's gone. He will tell you blandly that a man with his large frame can carry a lot of weight without being fat and a mere two hundred and forty pounds is about right for him."

"That would seem to be Mr. Pilcher," Kate said.

"The Mrs. Pilcher type comes down to the beach now and then too," I mused, "though not as much as she used to, I guess, before those hips began to build. And she'll spend more time under the umbrella than she did last year and eat a few less hamburgers. You'll see her arrive in a bigger and better car, more than likely, as years go by. And one day she'll give up the battle entirely and eat a double chocolate marshmallow sundae whenever she wants it and let a fifty dollar corset or a forty-dollar swim suit do all her worrying. Any additions, Kate?"

"None. I'm getting a liberal education in beaches and the people who go there. Please go on."

"Sure," I said. "As long as we're just kidding around I'll carry the ball one more time. The doctor. Cronk, I think they introduced him. Dr. Cronk."

"This should be good," Kate laughed. "He hasn't been in and he didn't bring a bathing suit. How do you classify him on the Bowman beach scale?"

"He comes out all right, as long as there isn't anything specific to nail him on. He doesn't give a damn about the water and what's more, he doesn't care who knows it. From here we see a somewhat nervous gent in his fifties. Rimless glasses, a round face, no tan. He's a little belligerent, I'd guess—a little too forceful about not letting anyone get him to paddle around in the pool. That Lincoln outside must be his and means he probably takes in a tidy little sum in fees each year. I presume that reasonable intelligence and ability will have to be credited to him, if he's made it through the rough deal that medical school is said to be. He reads the daily paper with gusto and probably stays away from the people he reads about." I grinned and added: "As far as the Bowman beach scale goes, we'll say Dr. Cronk is at least honest. We see him seldom and then only when the family drags him along by the collar. Which brings a question to mind. Have you run into him up here before?"

"Once. Last spring, I think. I can't be sure. Not with his family, though, if he has any."

I shifted to a more comfortable position and fixed a steady eye on the girl. "So far I've been on safe ground. You don't know these three any better than I do. Or very little, but you do know George and Sandy, so how about a blonde's eye view on the lord of the manor? What about George?"

Kate let a twinkle work its way into her eye and then a smile broke over her tan face. "That hardly seems fair—you should take a flyer on George, too, just to show me that Bowman knows his beach people. Where do we put George Engle?"

I looked over toward my smokes and matches across the pool. A stall. Three minutes, maybe, to think of something. "Time out," I grinned. "I'll get my cigarettes and be back."

The blonde watched me go and I didn't hurry any. I had already had a few ideas about the pool. Now I watched Engle. He stood by the diving board, a trim, well-formed man who had taken the best possible care of his physical being. Fifty, Kate had said, and I thought now that she'd given him the benefit of a good five years. Fifty-five, say, with straight gray hair that hadn't yet made him a highbrow. He was as tan as walnut stain and it made his teeth flash white when he smiled.

I picked up my pack and matches and started back. Small black tile numbers just below the water level marked the fifteen foot depth under the board and it graded up to three feet, the dark numbers waving slightly as the tiny ripples on the water distorted them. Fifteen feet of water under a low board—and it told me something else about Engle. I walked slowly back to the pad, flopped down, offered smokes, and looked at Kate.

"Here it is," I said lightly. "We'll try one for size on George Engle. Apart from age and the rest that's visible, I'd say George hasn't always been a swimming enthusiast. In fact he's only been a water bug for three or four years, Kate. Right?"

Her eyes came up a little and she nodded slowly.

"Uh-huh." I said, gaining confidence. "He took it up, probably because Sandy liked to swim, but like some of the people who join a church to please a bride, George really got interested. Now he loves the pool. As far as being a husband goes, George would stop at nothing in his efforts to please Sandy. He's considerate, a good provider, well mannered, and yet has enough determination and force to keep from being a milktoast. Okay so far?"

"I'm trying to remember," Kate said, "what I might have said that told you George didn't swim much before he met Sandy. I mean—"

"Elementary, my dear Watson," I grinned. "No one puts this much cash into a pool without professional advice. Any pool man would have told him that six to eight feet is enough under a low board. It goes up—or down really—to fifteen feet for a tower but there is no tower here. So probably George had the pool built for maximum depth and figured to put the tower in later. In fact the base plates for a tower are already in the concrete. Now, I ask myself, why didn't he put it in when the pool was made? Surely money was no problem. And that leads us to a very fine point about George Engle. He didn't want a tower to dive from until he became an expert on the rest of it—the springboard and swimming in general. Because G.E. is a man who makes sure that he always looks good. Unlike Pilcher who wishes he did."

"All right, Sherlock, I'll buy that," Kate laughed. "And I'm sorry to have put you on the spot."

"You can do penance," I said lightly. "You can take over the opium pipe for a while and do a little dreaming for me. You were very insistent, Kate, that Gregory provide you with a man who would be at home in the water. But look at what's here—Pilcher who splashes more than he swims, Dr. Cronk who hasn't even pulled on a bathing suit, and a host who is an ardent fan but no better than a fair swimmer, and that in an elderly sort of way. True, you're an expert. I'm not simonizing the apple when I say you're really good. But what about Sandy Engle? As a kid she was nuts about the water, you tell me. Now I see her as strictly a dry number. She hasn't gotten wet once, and while I'm a big boy now and don't go around asking girls why they can't go swimming, I get the feeling this has nothing to do with the calendar. I'm willing to bet she doesn't swim any more. Period. What's the pitch, Kate? Does she or doesn't she?"

"Well, yes and no, Marty."

"That's an answer?"

"I mean she has been in. I've seen her, but late at night. Mostly it's as you say. She stays on the patio lounge or lies in the grass. But a few times I've been awake in the night and looking down from my window I've watched Sandy and George swim."

"No one else around. You didn't join them?"

"No. It was almost obvious that she didn't care to be in while the rest of us were and that's another reason I wanted to get someone to come up here and look things over."

"It's your money," I told her. "How late was this swimming party for two?"

Kate thought a moment. "Perhaps one-thirty in the morning. Or almost, because the caretaker was getting ready to drain the pool and wash it down. He does that around two every morning, I think George told me."

I smoked in silence and hoped I looked like a man thinking about something but for the life of me I couldn't tie into anything concrete. An occasional dip in the moonlight, that I could understand. But usually people who go for that kind of diversion are crazy about the water—or each other—and in view of what Kate had told me it was hard to tell which was right.

"You did say George was in too. I mean, it wasn't just Sandy swimming and George watching, Kate?"

"No. No, both of them were in. I watched for several minutes."

I gave it more silence, and somewhere there the thing died. A wave of doubts began to set in. About myself. Maybe Gregory had guessed this was nothing serious and had sent a boy to do a man's work. Maybe this called for experience and know-how in the art of investigation and maybe I was letting everybody down, including myself. I smoked and tried to think but before me was the thin veil of something only dimly seen and a little beyond my reach. My fingers scraped against the concrete deck of the pool and I clamped my teeth tightly together. I wasn't quite sure how, but I was determined that one way or another I was going to keep a sharp eye peeled in Kate Weston's interests, no matter how she finally fit in. Mentally I ran over the others—the pudgy Pilcher and his brown-haired, heavy-hipped wife. George Engle, fit and fiftyish, who had a wife under thirty. And the wife,

Sandy Engle, thin, dark and lovely in an abnormally retiring way. Dr. Cronk, staying strictly dry in a place
where swimming was the main course.

Then I looked up and something new had been added.
Something with red hair and a figure that could have been
a model's stock in trade stood near the diving board and
chatted idly with George Engle. I touched a hand to the
tan shoulder beside me.

"A late arrival, Kate. Know this one?"

She rolled lazily onto her side, then opened a sleepy
eye. Then she opened both eyes and sat up. "No, Marty,
this one I haven't seen before. My God. Competition has
increased. I can see that from here."

"Competition?"

"The eligible males in this camp are, for the most part,
few and far between."

I resisted the obvious and together Kate and I watched
the redhead. She hadn't gotten into her bathing suit yet.
George led her toward the terrace side of the pool to
introduce the other guests and I tried to size her up—
well-filled nylons, yellow skirt cut as high as Schiaparelli
would allow, sweater tight in just the right places. She
walked with a trace of charm school in her step, but
the lessons had been a long time ago because when she
and Engle came around to our side and I got to my feet
for the introductions I saw a few more years in her face
than I'd seen in her construction. I mentally moved her
from the last of the teens on into middle twenties.

"Miss Doyle. Miss Weston and Mr. Bowman," George
said. I nodded and was paid off with a warm smile and
frank appraisal. The redhead gave Kate a smile too, but
one cut from different cloth.

"You may have caught one of Miss Doyle's pictures
last month," George Engle said easily. "She's a starlet on
her way up. Elsa Doyle. Your latest was *Alone At Night,*
wasn't it, Elsa?"

"Oh?" I said. Kate raised an interested eyebrow and I thought that Elsa's brief glance at George Engle carried something less than appreciation for the plug. And I wondered why, because with TV cutting into the box office more every day, movie people shy away from publicity like a hungry kid passes up an ice cream cone on a hot afternoon.

Engle didn't leave it there. "We're expecting great things for Elsa," he said. "Naturally there are a lot of pitfalls for show people, but barring accidents she should go far. We're certainly going to keep our fingers crossed for her."

"Thanks, George." She said it with measured politeness and favored him with a smile that was just a shade short of being sincere. We made pleasantries for another few minutes, then watched the pair of them walk along the narrow band of concrete between the side of the pool and high Italian cypress as they went toward the house. I flopped down on the green pad again, lit a fresh smoke and tried to read something into George Engle's crack about pitfalls and accidents. Engle had much better manners than to mention something like that without a reason. His tone had been a little like talking to a friend in a hospital bed, telling him you hope he'll recover, and then recalling that you've known several others who had his same malady, God rest their souls.

Four

EVENING BROUGHT dinner on the terrace, two tables of bridge, and early good nights. At eleven o'clock I leaned on the window sill of one of George Engle's guest rooms and watched thin trails of vapor caught in the moonlight falling across the upper reservoir. A narrow walk circled the building on the side toward the hill and, stepping outside, I struck a match, touched off a final smoke before hitting the sack, and listened to the small noises of the desert night. When I ground out the red ember and went inside, I piled my change on the dresser, slipped off my watch, and climbed out of my pants. There was a silver dollar among the coins I'd shelled out and I tossed and caught it and, without even glancing to see whether it was heads or tails, reached for a pair of swimming trunks.

The pool was deserted. Good enough. You get a lot of swimming on the beach but your diving tapers off and I needed a little work to put me in shape before the inn opened at Death Valley, so I stepped onto the board and led off with a simple jackknife. Not good. I repeated, this time going almost to the bright, sunken stainless steel drain grill fifteen feet below. Then a couple more, going as shallow as I could, and after that a full gainer or two.

"Very good, Mr. Bowman."

I turned to see George Engle standing behind me. "Thanks," I said, and stepped down from the board. "Next?"

"No. You go ahead. I'd like to learn to do that half as well as you do, Marty."

"Thanks again," I said. "Takes a little patience, I guess, but that's about all."

"I doubt that," Engle said good-naturedly. "I get all the practice one man can stand, yet improvement seems to come slowly."

"Take a couple," I said. "I'll watch and see if we can't speed the process a little."

His pleasure was genuine and for twenty minutes George Engle dove and I worked with him. A diligent pupil and one determined to turn in a creditable performance. You don't find many like that—at any age. I thought about his young wife and how hard Engle must

have worked to stay trim and fit and all and I wanted to
help him improve his diving. But another thing I've found
is that there comes a time when the best thing you can
do for a person who's trying to learn is let him alone.
When G.E. reached that point I slung my towel across
my shoulders and started an exit.

"Watching you work is making me hungry," I said.
"I seem to remember your mentioning an all-night serve-
yourself snack bar somewhere in the house."

"By all means," he said. He walked along a few steps
and gestured toward the door near one end. "Straight
through to the kitchen. Make yourself at home and I'll
be along in a few minutes."

"Thanks," I said, then looked up sharply as something
splashed back in the pool.

George smiled. "Damn bugs. Every once in a while a
big one will see those lights under the water and fly
toward it."

I muttered an "Oh," and toddled off to the groceries.
Provisions for midnight chow were on par with the rest of
the Engle layout. I laid out two slices of bread, then went
eny-meeny-miney-moe among the assortment of meats,
cheeses and relish arranged nearby, and came up with
something in the nature of a Dagwood Special. Drawing
a cup of coffee, I sat down to munch my sandwich and
browse through the magazine rack.

The stock of literature ran mostly to men's mags with
a liberal sprinkling of physical-culture stuff. I thumbed
around a while, then started an article on muscle tone
but when I came to the continued part it said turn to
page ninety-six. There wasn't one. It was the last sheet,
next to the cover, and someone had torn it out. Very
vexing. Out of idle curiosity, I pulled the issue before
mine and the three that followed it. All of them had a
page ninety-six and every one of those pages had the
same advertisement on the back side. I grinned then,

because the page that had been carefully cut out was one of those "do-you-long-for-your-youthful-vigor" booby traps that advise you to waste no time in sending the enclosed coupon along with four dollars. Dr. Holcum's pills, according to the ad, would indeed put you back in the saddle again. It looked like one or another of Engle's previous guests was in the market for hormone shots.

I downed the rest of my coffee, glanced at the wall clock, then decided that George had had more than a half hour to work on his dives and maybe I ought to drop by and see if he was doing all right. A light wind had started to blow down from the hill. I went across the terrace separating the pool from the rambling, U-shaped house. Engle wasn't in sight. He didn't bob up while I watched and I guessed he'd called it a night so I turned toward the walk leading to my own room, then stopped and whirled around like you do when your mind has just caught up with something your eyes have seen.

A towel and a robe draped across the back of a lawn chair near the diving board. I broke into a jog. When I neared the pool the black tile numbers caught my eye— a one and a five standing motionless against their background of blue. Then I saw something else. The still form of George Engle rested on the bottom under fifteen feet of water.

I gave a king-sized yell and plunged in.

Five

HE LAY face down, his gray hair straggling away in all directions from the top of his head, and there wouldn't be that problem of a struggling victim. A practiced routine. Straight to the bottom, slip an arm across one shoulder and under the arm on the other side, the quick hard push against the tile under foot, and a few strong strokes to the top. I tugged Engle to a ladder, shifted his body, and carried him up the steps and over to the grass. Putting him face down again, I lifted his middle a couple of times, then jammed his hands under his cheek, knelt and leaned forward to press on his back and ribs. Behind me I heard the pad of running feet and shouts and questions filled the night. I went to work in the steady rhythmic pace. Both hands against his ribs as I came forward to press against his lungs, then slip the hands off and out to his bent elbows to pull up and towards me in an effort to start his breathing.

Kate arrived first, but in just a few seconds we had a full house. Sandy Engle on her knees beside George, her hand stroking his wet hair. Flopping robes and pajama-clad legs all around, and someone asked where Dr. Cronk was. He stepped out from behind the Pilchers and bent over our host.

"Hell, he's a doctor," Pilcher said significantly. "Let him handle it, Bowman."

I glanced at Sandy Engle. She looked at Cronk and he looked at me. I stood up. "He's yours, doc," I said.

But I couldn't stay out of it. Not for long, because if George Engle wasn't already dead he would be soon. Cronk slid a hand under Engle's face and held it there while he looked thoughtful. "No pulse," he said.

"Look, doc, he was in the pool. On the bottom. I don't know how long but that's where I found him, so let's give him some artificial respiration. Time's wasting."

"It won't help, Bowman." Dr. Cronk shook his head slowly. "Heart. Bad case, really. George has been lucky to stay with us this long."

"This you can tell from feeling a pulse that isn't there?"

"I'm familiar with his case, Bowman."

I looked at Kate beside me, then back to Cronk still

squatting by Engle. "Don't you give some kind of a shot for heart attack?" I asked.

"Fact is, I'm up here on sort of a vacation. Don't even have a bag in the car, I'm afraid. Not that it would do any good. You see—"

"I see a man who might live with a little help," I cut in, dropping down again. "You tend to his heart, doc, and I'll work on his respiration, huh? And someone get a blanket."

I went back to work, matching the cycle of artificial respiration to the speed of my own breathing. Sandy was still beside George, her long black hair falling almost to his back as she bent over him and as I worked I glanced around at the slippered feet and paired pajama legs that ringed us in. Kate just behind me, and the Pilchers. Dr. Cronk had stood up again and a bit farther back I saw the shoes and pants legs of the Philippino gardener and man of all work. Beside him was his wife, a silent woman whose age would have been hard to guess. On the other side and apart from the others was the redhead who'd arrived in the evening.

Forward, pressure on the ribs, slide the hands off and pull George's elbows back on the return—and hope it would pay off. No telling how long he'd been in the water. Anything up to half an hour. But it could be a lot less and as long as there was a spark of hope I intended to keep trying. And thinking.

Glancing up now and then I tried to read something into the faces around me. Anxiety? Yes, a measure of that. And a certain amount of fear—you always see that near an accident of any kind. People seem to be mentally placing themselves in the victim's shoes and it isn't a pleasant feeling. But in a family group you'll find some semblance of sadness or pity or sorrow when disaster strikes and we were notably short on that at the moment. To me George Engle was strictly a man I'd pulled out of the water. I've never lost one at a pool because there you can keep track and get 'em before they've been under more than a few seconds but at the beach it's different. Some you bring around and some you have to send away to the coroner and it can't be helped, but you can feel sorry for another human who's had tough luck and that's how I've always felt. Yet looking around me I couldn't help thinking that there wasn't a person here as concerned as I was about the life of George Engle.

Pilcher had admonished me to turn things over to Dr. Cronk. And Cronk was willing to write G.E. off as beyond hope. Sandy Engle. No tears, but sometimes that's the bitterest kind of grief. I couldn't be sure. Kate? She was behind me—I would have had to stop work to see her face. Mrs. Pilcher. Heavy and a little dull around the eyes. I had the feeling that if someone passed sandwiches she'd take one and munch absently as she waited to hear that it was all over and why don't we get some sleep.

And on the other side—silk pajamas red enough to delight the heart of a true party member, white bedroom slippers that could quite well have been used in a film at one time or another, and a wrap-around robe which had a carelessness about its style that only a lot of time and money can create.

And a body not yet breathing by itself.

By the time I'd worked ten minutes on Engle I was beginning to get the idea. I looked up and Kate's eyes met mine.

"You'd best take Sandy inside," I suggested quietly.

Kate nodded and put an arm around Sandy Engle. I waited until they were halfway to the house, then turned to Cronk.

"Call the sheriff's office. We aren't going to be lucky this time, I guess."

Cronk looked at Pilcher, then back to me. "That won't

be necessary, Bowman. I'm a member of the medical profession and I'll sign the death certificate."

I worked along a few more seconds. "Look, doc, you're a little confused. This is an accidental death, not a natural one. It has to be reported, remember? So let's someone get to a phone. The operator will connect you to the nearest sub-station. I'll work a while longer but we'd better let the law in on this as quickly as possible." Once again we put it to a vote as Cronk looked toward Pilcher. Then the three of them, Pilcher, his wife, and the doc went toward the house. Elsa Doyle stayed. We had Engle under the blanket and I kept up the continuous effort to start his breathing again.

"He's dead. I mean he hasn't any real chance at all, has he, Mr. Bowman?"

"Very little." I said it slowly and then looked up to see how she was taking it. We had it now. Everything—tears, the handkerchief pressed tightly to her cheeks, a half-silent tremble—straight from the death scene of a heavy melodrama film. Good—but a little late. It made me sore.

"Run up to the house and see if you can help Kate take care of Sandy," I said sharply. When she was gone I settled into the routine and let my mind dig around the edges for a while. Mrs. Pilcher must have decided to stay indoors but before long Pilcher and Doc Cronk returned to keep me company while we waited for the sheriff. It was a full half hour more before we heard the siren winding up toward the Engle estate, and when we did Cronk and Pilcher hurried toward the entrance to form a reception committee of two.

I watched them stride across the lawn from the house, two tall men, one a bit more husky than the other, and flanked by Pilcher and the doc. They, too, had a routine. The heavier of the two bent toward Engle's face, held a light, and rolled the eyelid back. He watched for several seconds, then shook his head.

"Fair enough," I said, getting to my feet. "It never hurts to try."

"Mr. Toland," Cronk said quickly. "He's deputy sheriff from Newhall station. And Mr. Widdle. Mr. Bowman."

I shook hands with Toland and Widdle. Toland was the husky one, late forties, maybe, and you wouldn't want to spit in his eye just for kicks. He had that rugged look that goes with a leathery hide and broad frame. Slow and easy. He looked you over with a cool eye that was appraising and yet not offensive, somehow. You got the feeling that he could probably work all day and still roll out at three ayem for a tramp through the hills in search of deer. The outdoors man. His assistant was younger and probably more eager, but he hid it well. He gave me a smile with his handshake, then glanced apologetically toward the blanket and grew serious again. You could call them a pair of honest Westerners, I guess.

"We'll have to get the details straight," Toland said smoothly. "The time and things like that. The coroner will be along later and we'd best not move Mr. Engle again." Toland bent to pull the blanket a little farther up and covered the face, then nodded toward the deck chairs. We sat down.

"Take a few minutes to collect yourselves," he advised us, "while I look this pool over. Never been on the grounds myself, but I've seen her from the hill above. Several times." He went toward the shallow end, then around on the narrow ribbon of cement bordering the eucalyptus. At the diving board he stopped to look for a while, then came over and sat down on a patio type chaise lounge. He found a pencil and a small notebook and spread it out on the low coffee table.

"Routine, gentlemen, but required by law. Now as Dr. Cronk says, these heart cases sometimes have an attack while swimming. If no one's around, it's unfortunate, but that's the way things are. A man can't live under glass all his life, can he now?"

Pilcher allowed that the sheriff was right.

"Who saw him last?"

There was a silence. I broke it with, "Unless someone was here when he went under and stayed there, how would you know if you were the last to see George alive?"

"Okay," Toland said good-naturedly. "Who saw Mr. Engle in the last hour before he was found? And who found him, by the way?"

"I win both times," I said. Then I told them about George practicing his dives and how I left him and went for a sandwich. That brought it up to where the others came in.

"Uh-huh. And Dr. Cronk states that the deceased had a bad heart, and that it was the cause of death. Engle being found on the bottom of a pool, though, we'd best consider drowning as a possibility. I don't know. Maybe when the coroner gets a look—"

"Frank!"

Toland snapped his head around and we all looked toward the blanket over George Engle. Widdle knelt by the body, the corner of the blanket folded back. "Better have a look, Frank." he said, and then as some of us got up to tag along Widdle added: "Alone."

Frank Toland stopped and motioned us back. "Wait there for me." Then he went over to his assistant. The pair of them bent over Engle for several minutes and when they put the blanket back Toland's look had changed considerably.

"Quite a pool," he said tightly, seating himself again. "In fact this whole layout is pretty fancy. Engle had a great deal of money, I'd guess."

No one said a word. It was obvious that Toland no longer intended to indulge that buddy-buddy attitude toward us.

"Yeah, you can see it on all sides. Money. So much of it that Engle came to love the feel of the stuff, I guess."

"I don't quite follow you, Sheriff," Cronk said. He found a wrinkled handkerchief, slipped off his glasses, and began to polish them. Watching closely, I caught a hint of anxiety in his eyes.

Toland drummed heavy fingers on the metal coffee table. He looked first at me, then toward Cronk and Pilcher. Getting up, Toland went to Engle's robe and towel draped over the deck chair and made a careful search of both pockets. When he came back to us he shook his head.

"The more I see of this the less I like it," he said firmly. "Bob, you stay here with Engle until the coroner comes. The rest of us will go up to the house and sweat it out. I want to make a phone call or two, then maybe have a word with each of you. And Mrs. Engle."

He turned toward the house and we followed along in silence. Engle's combination houseboy and gardener had built a fire and shortly he came in with a setup for coffee all around. Toland sent for the women, then trailed down the hall after the Philippino.

He was gone quite a while. Pilcher and Cronk appropriated the leather sofa near the fireplace and when Pilcher's wife came in she joined them. They held a low-voiced huddle. Elsa Doyle swept in like a movie queen going on set and I guessed that she'd spent the last half hour running a comb through the twenty-dollar henna job she was sporting, and maybe seeing that the seams of the stockings she'd managed to slip on were straight. She found a chair near mine and offered smokes. I took one. When Kate came in I made a place for her on the other side.

"What's happening, Marty? I thought Dr. Cronk said—"

"The sheriff found something," I cut in. "He won't say what but somehow it's changed things."

Elsa Doyle ran a practiced hand through her red hair. "He thinks George was—murdered?"

"He's doing some checking," I hedged. Elsa passed a smoke to Kate and we waited for the return of the law. When he finally got back to us he'd managed to regain his former easy attitude.

"Routine," he said again. "Just getting things lined out. Now we've established that Bowman saw Engle about a half hour before he went into the pool. Or rather a half hour before he was found dead. Who saw him after Bowman went for that sandwich?"

We had several seconds of silence while each of us glanced around the room. "Come, come," Toland urged. "Someone must have dropped by the pool after Bowman left. Think hard now. That would have been between eleven-thirty and midnight, roughly."

"Uh-huh," he said softly when it became obvious that he had no takers on his first try. "Well, next we ought to sort of get it straight who's who and why you're here. We can start with Dr. Cronk. How long has Engle had a heart condition, doctor, before we go into the rest?"

"I wouldn't know without consulting my records."

"But you were treating him?"

"As a matter of fact I didn't say that George was under my care," Cronk said stiffly. Watching him I could see that "we-professional-men" attitude building in his face. He was getting ready to hide behind that and he didn't like being questioned by Sheriff Toland. "I merely mentioned that I was aware of Engle's heart ailment. My practice isn't here, but in San Diego."

"You said you'd check your records, Doctor," Toland reminded him mildly.

"One examination. It was years ago, but I can look it up."

"Maybe we'll ask you to do that later," Toland said blandly. "Now as I get it, you're up here as a guest. Just a personal friend of Engle. That it?"

"That's right, Sheriff."

"And how about you two?" Toland asked, turning toward the Pilchers. "Just weekending here?"

"Yes." In the absence of a toothpick, Pilcher had found a blade of grass and now it was firmly rooted between his thick lips.

"What do you do, Mr. Pilcher?"

"Wholesale supply. Metals. That type of thing."

"Where?"

"Los Angeles."

"Uh-huh. And now Mr. Bowman." I saw Pilcher's heavy wife tilt her nose a little higher as all eyes turned my way. But I wasn't worried. I just told him about being a lifeguard and where I'd worked and a lot of other things he could check. Then I tapered the end of it and fit it into being a friend of Miss Weston and said I'd come up for a few days as sort of a guest of a guest. In a way it was a little humorous, because I knew that the blonde thought I was dishing out a phoney background. She must have thought that Gregory's agency provided their men with an airtight backdrop.

"A lifeguard. Maybe you can help us, Bowman. You saw George Engle swimming earlier in the day?"

"We all did. He was fond of the water and went in often."

"Sure, sure." Toland was patient but determined. He gave me a smile and said, "Still, you being a professional around pools, I'd like your opinion. Would you say that Engle could have just up and drowned himself?"

"You're forgetting the heart, Sheriff."

"That's the doctor's angle," Toland said easily. "I

want to know what Bowman thinks."

"He was a good swimmer. Damn good, for a man his age. But most of the people who drown in the surf are strong swimmers, Sheriff. Anyone can get a cramp. Anyone can bump his head on the bottom of a pool and pass out in the water. If no one happens to see him, it's just tough. Still, you've got no worries, Toland. The autopsy will show whether he drowned, or not."

Toland put a heavy thumb to his chin and thought a moment, then let me off of the hook. With a few pointed and direct questions he established that the servants were both in their own quarters, the man of all work resting before his nightly session of draining and filling the plunge, his wife off for the day. From Elsa Doyle, Toland got a production. He tried to shut off the publicity campaign several times but she gave him every detail—childhood to her latest "achievement" —the reluctance to push herself I'd noted earlier had vanished since George Engle was no longer with us. I wondered about that as we listened to her life story. And it wasn't without interest entirely. She'd worked as a bathing cutie and decorative ornament in the Florida cypress gardens as a teen-ager. Then into a USO show five years ago and from there to the films. About what the publicity department would whip up for any other starlet they were promoting. It made good copy.

That left Kate and when Toland asked what she did for a living she touched a tongue to her lips and watched me while she answered.

"I work in women's apparel. Weston's. It's in Hollywood, Mr. Toland."

"Oh?" He said it lightly and I was thinking about a lot of things just then. The big Cad she drove and those fancy clothes. Pretty lucky, this kid. Her family owning a clothing shop and all. She was probably assistant manager or some other such title and it reminded me of the guy who said he started at the bottom of the company and in six weeks worked his way up to first vice president. Owed his success, he claimed, to hard work, diligent attention to detail, study, and the fact that his father owned the business. Now, watching Kate answer Toland's questions, I had to admit to a small bit of envy for some of those money families.

There wasn't anything I hadn't found out on the trip up here, and when Toland finished with Kate he favored us all with a kindly look. "Everything seems all right except one little item, folks." He swung back to me and added, "I guess we can clear that up in short order, Bowman. It looks like you were the last to see Engle alive. Teaching him to dive, you said. Anything special about his dives?"

"No. Just a simple jackknife."

"And how do you practice a jackknife?"

I met his eyes and said, "Can you give me a little more on that? Exactly what do you want to know, Sheriff?"

"Where the money comes in, Bowman."

"What money?"

"Engle had a coin in his hand when he died. It's still there. He wouldn't need that to practice a dive, would he?"

"Hell, no. But he might have gotten one out of his pocket to horse around a little. Kids dive for bottle caps. Maybe Engle was diving for a coin."

"There aren't any others in his robe pocket, Bowman. And when I talked to his missus a few minutes ago she didn't recall that he's ever been addicted to diving for coins."

"Include me, Sheriff," I grinned. "You're the one that's talking about money. I didn't see Engle have any either."

"Well, we'll see. I guess—" He broke off as the sound of a heavy car laboring up the grade came through to us. "Excuse me, folks," he said. "I'll be back directly.

It might be a good idea for all of you to be around as I'll probably want to see you later."

"Mind if I change to some clothes?" I asked, pointing to my bathing trunks. "This looks like a long night coming up."

"Go ahead, Bowman. And come back, huh?"

Then he was gone. I glanced at Kate and said, "You heard the man. I'll be right back."

Walking down the corridor, I turned into my room, shucked out of the still damp trunks, and stepped into the shower. Cold water spattered over me as I went over the details at hand. So maybe Engle had pushed off before his time and one of those gathered was strictly dangerous people. But who? And why? I toweled myself, pulled out clean shorts, climbed into slacks and found a sport shirt. Socks and shoes, and then I combed my hair and went over to the dresser to put on my watch and scoop the change into my pocket.

But I didn't touch my money. Instead I stood for several seconds looking at the top of the dresser. Then I pulled it away from the wall and got down on my hands and knees for a search of the rug, but I didn't find anything. Standing up again, I pushed the dresser back and felt for my cigarettes. Now I knew about the coin in George Engle's hand.

My silver dollar was missing.

Six

FUMBLING THROUGH my pockets, I came up with a match and struck a light. *Easy, boy,* I told myself. *Let's be sure.* I laid the cigarette on the edge of a glass ashtray and got down on all fours again. No luck. Then I went through my other pants, knowing by now that it was a waste of time. My silver buck was gone. Picking up my smoke, I went to the door leading out to the narrow walk on the side toward the hill. I hadn't snapped the lock on that door. Someone had been watching. Someone saw me go for the swim and someone made a short tour through my room and picked up the silver dollar.

I smoked in the darkness and thought about it for a while. Toland was going to try to run that coin to earth and he'd certainly end up pointing the finger at me. Six possibilities on who could have pushed Engle over the line and a thousand on how it was done. Dive in after him and hold him under. A strong swimmer could have done that—the cypress along the far side would have been ample hiding place to wait for the right moment. Wrap a beach towel over a hammer or pipe or any heavy object and you have another way. Tap Engle on the head and boost his unconscious body in to drown. But in any case, fold those brown fingers around that silver dollar of Bowman's. Sure, they had to have a fall guy from somewhere and I'd been elected. But I had one advantage. Toland was still in doubt; I was sure it was murder and it would give me a head start.

My cigarette was burning low. I dropped it on the concrete, stepped on it, and went back inside. In a drawer I found some paper and a pencil. I laid out six sheets and wrote a name on the top of each. Dan Pilcher, Mrs. Pilcher, Dr. Cronk, Elsa Doyle, Sandy Engle, and Kate Weston. I thought about the two servants, then decided against including their names. There was going to be little enough I could find out about the others and if the Philippino or his wife were trying to get rid of George Engle—well, I could add a couple of slips if anything in the way of evidence came up. The pressing need of the moment was to get something worth while on the six I had. One by one I dropped them on the bed. Kate. Kate, the only one for which I had a single item. Kate Weston had felt that something was wrong. She had brought me up here to help her find out about Sandy Engle.

Or maybe to be an alibi.

I folded the sheets together and went back down to the Engle living room, my mind made up that one of the six was going to have to be promoted. Marty Bowman didn't enjoy being the number one candidate and as of the moment that's exactly what he was.

I breezed into the living room to the babble of half a dozen voices but as soon as they saw me the room quieted down. It happens to everyone at some time or another and there are several ways to handle a situation like that. I stood there and waited for someone to come to life and suddenly three or four of them started talking at once. I put on my best grin and walked toward the fireplace.

"Let's talk about it, people," I said. "What's the beef?"

"Some of our friends were pointing out that no one actually saw you bring George out of the pool, Marty. We've been having a small hassel," Kate said.

I looked around and felt for my smokes. "True enough. So where does that lead? I'm willing to listen. Someone have an idea?"

Pilcher opened his fat face, then changed his mind and looked away. His wife blurted out, "You said he was diving when you went for a sandwich, Mr. Bowman. How do we know that you didn't knock him unconscious and push him into the water?"

"A good question. And how do I know that one of you didn't tap George on the head and do the same? The row of cypress is only a few feet from the pool on one side, remember. There is a good half hour unaccounted for, and any one of you could have been standing behind those trees when I left Engle to his dives."

Dr. Cronk shifted in his chair and pointed a thick finger at me. "But you, Mr. Bowman, insisted on artificial respiraton. A lot of it, even after competent medical judgment pronounced George dead. Could it be that you were hiding something?"

"What can you hide with artificial respiration?"

"Plenty, Bowman. For one thing, any little bits of skin or a few hairs or such that they might find on Engle, and trace to you would now be explained. You worked on him."

"Well, I guess—"

"And another thing. Suppose you did strangle him or jam a knee into his stomach or any one of a number of things. The marks would be gone. Over forty minutes you pushed him back and forth down there on the grass. Any tell-tale redness in the solar plexus, bruises along the neck, marks of violence of any kind would be lost in the shuffle. Very cleverly obliterated, Bowman." Cronk sat back in his chair and gave me a "let's-see-you-wiggle-out-of-that" glare as he applied a fresh handkerchief to the lenses of his glasses.

"You forget," Kate said firmly, "that a motive is lacking."

"As it is for all of us, my dear," Mrs. Pilcher put in sweetly.

"Hell, yes," Pilcher grunted. "None of us had any reason to do George in."

I didn't have an answer ready for Doc Cronk but I could silence our fat friend Pilcher. I gave him an innocent grin and said, "Hell of a note, isn't it?"

"What?"

"Nobody's got a motive. We just come up here to smell the sagebrush. Or at least some of us do. Remember?"

That cooled his coffee. He'd said too much down in

front of the café earlier in the day, made it clear he was coming up here against his will. He didn't particularly enjoy my tossing his words back at him. I stared hard at him and he looked away. I wondered what he'd shell out to have those words back again.

It occurred to me that one member of the wake hadn't said anything yet and I looked across at the redhead. The quiet type tonight. She certainly had her moods. I made a mental tabulation of them. She'd been reticent when George Engle introduced her and plugged her career. I'd had her for a bridge partner earlier during the evening and you couldn't ask for a more cool or clever player—she'd stuck strictly to the percentages and we'd come out on the long side of the ledger. Then a full scale color production when the sheriff took her history. Now she was sitting back to listen while we harped at one another.

You could safely say that Elsa Doyle had a lot more sense then most good young starlets are supposed to possess. I was working on a way to drag her into our huddle when Toland came into the room.

"The coroner's taking Engle down for an autopsy. We'll call in the morning and it would help if one of you will sort of prepare Mrs. Engle so she'll be able to tell us whom she wants to handle the rites.

"So far we're going to say he drowned when a heart attack caught him in the pool. Strictly tentative. All of you have said you're here for the weekend, so I won't have to make you stay. It might look bad, though, if after planning to be here a couple of days you suddenly remember pressing business in the city. You get my point?"

He drew several nods and no objections. "Good. I'm glad you're cooperating. And I have one more detail. If no one has anything against it, I'd like to take prints.

When I phoned I had Ed—he's doing the coroner work for us this year—stop by my office and bring the works. So if you'll let me have your fingers here for a second—"

Toland had plenty of brains behind that weather-beaten face of his. He'd gone ahead on the assumption that no one would object and he hadn't exactly given anyone a chance to refuse. Twenty minutes later he said good night, reminded us that he hoped we'd all be a-round in the morning, and let himself out. There wasn't any good reason for starting the bickering over again. I had a few ideas myself, but there would be time enough later to go into the Pilcher-Cronk friendship. Instead I thought about the doctor and his quick and final judgment on Engle, and most of all I thought about the things he didn't do.

Those summers in the lifeguard tower, again. You pull someone out and go to work, but the call is sent and in short order you get equipment and a doctor on the scene. And he doesn't grab someone's wrist and say let's go home. Not by a long shot. You get activity, but good. From Cronk we got a performance that a first class boy scout would have been ashamed of. I rubbed my chin and thought about that a while, and then I looked at Kate.

"Let's get some air, shall we?" She stood up, but before I turned away I said to Cronk, "I hear there's a good moonlight view of the valley from one of these paths. Place called McBurney's point. You know where it is, Doc?"

"No."

That was short and final but I gave it one more boost. "I thought maybe being up here before you might be familiar with it. Doesn't it strike a chord?"

"No. Never heard of it and I'm certainly not going in search of it tonight, Bowman."

I nodded to Kate and we went toward the door. Bright moonlight falling on the hillside flooded the grounds and lit the concrete walk leading toward the plunge. We stopped some distance away and watched the gardener at work, and I glanced at my watch.

"Two o'clock, Kate. I guess you could say the staff here is well trained." She looked up at me and we went on toward the pool. It was empty now, and the Philippino, working in sneakers and faded denims was hosing down the bottom. A hazy vapor drifted up from the stream of water playing over blue tile and the film of brown melted away, swirled through the big stainless steel drainage grill and disappeared. We watched until he turned off the hose and went down the path to close the drain valve. A fresh supply of water began to splash into the clean pool. Kate took my arm and we walked on again.

"Marty, what do you think? I mean do you think George really had a heart attack?"

"Who can say?"

"In a way it looks bad. I went to the Gregory Agency and hired someone to come up here, and now George is dead. I know it would almost seem that I knew what was going to happen, but actually—"

"Sure," I said, and managed a reassuring pressure on her arm linked through mine.

After a while she said almost hesitantly, "Marty— did it appear to you that Dr. Cronk didn't really *want* to do anything for George? You tried, at least, but—"

"I know how it looks, Kate. But maybe the real reason Cronk didn't do something wasn't that he didn't want to."

"And?"

"The collection of people around this place puts a strain on your imagination, Kate. At least two of them are as phoney as a lead life preserver."

"Cronk?" she asked.

"I don't know what his name is," I said slowly, "but if he's a doctor I'm Esther Williams. I'm sure that one of the reasons he didn't do anything for George is that he didn't know what to do. No shot for the heart. No attempt even to see if George was breathing. He didn't even seem to know that all accidental deaths have to be reported." I stopped and faced her. "And one more thing. McBurney's point went over his head like a full moon. Didn't register. But any first-year medical student would have tumbled to that one. In fact you don't have to study medicine. There must be a million people who have had their apendixes chopped out and most of them would remember McBurney's point. It isn't out here; it's on your tummy. Between the hip bone and the navel on the right side. It's the place they press when they're deciding whether or not you're a candidate for an incision. Like to see my operation?"

"You think—"

"I don't know what I think—except that Cronk is not a doctor. Now why he should pose as one up here is hard to say. Maybe the answer to that would simplify things a little."

We started walking again, not saying anything for a few yards. Then she asked quietly, "You said there were two phonies—who's the other?"

"Me," I said miserably. "I'm not a detective. You're stuck with something left over from amateur night, Kate. The details I handed to Toland are the McCoy. I'm a beach boy or a life guard or a drifter from pool to pool or whatever you want to call me but as a detective, this is my first time out."

She didn't blow a gasket like I half expected her to. Instead she looked straight ahead, her arm still loosely

through mine. I found my smokes, lit a pair, and passed
one to her. She took it in silence and the ember glowed
momentarily as she inhaled. When she blew the smoke
out she said, "It beats me, Marty. Gregory's agency
has a quarter-page ad in the phone book. Domestic,
Marital, Criminal—every kind of service is listed. How
come?"

"I've been trying to figure. The way it looks to me is
that Gregory pegged this one as a blank, Kate. Maybe
he saw you drive up in seven thousand dollars worth of
chrome and gray leather, put it alongside your story
about a wife being held on the ranch, and came up with
much ado about nothing. He's a money-minded citizen,
Kate. He wouldn't let a fee escape without a struggle."

"But what about his regular operators?"

"You were choosey. You had to have someone who
would look right in that pool of Engle's. Gregory has
a good staff all right, but some of them are older
and some of them are fat and one I know carries his
teeth in his pocket except when his feet are under a table.
You didn't want anything like that; you'd made it pretty
plain. So the big man remembered Marty Bowman who
had asked for a job a couple of years before, and there
it is."

"I seem to remember something about him writing
checks to Bowman for twelve years," she said accusingly.

"I guess you do," I said, and told her about my
brother Fred and how I was tied in with the agency.
I finished with, "I'm not very proud of myself. I guess
everything except the actual words was a lie, Kate."

We smoked in silence, our slow steps taking us a-
long the tree-covered flagstone walk. The foliage was
heavy enough to block most of the moonlight and had
doubtlessly been set out to provide relief from the sun's
heat during the day. At the end of the path we paused

beside the huge valve which emptied Engle's pool into the lower reservoir and I put a foot on the iron crank
that served as a handle and looked across at Kate.

"Would you ask you what you're thinking if you were
me?" I grinned.

In the half light I saw a smile work its way into her
face. "I might."

"Good. I'll risk it. What's the word?"

"We got into this mess together. Let's dig in and see
if we can't work it out between us, Marty."

"Thanks. Thanks for not putting it on the 'make the
best of a bad bargain' level, Kate. And I hope you meant
it, because I'm going to lay everything I can right out
here in the open and start from there. You know the
coin Toland keeps harping about? Well, I'm afraid
that chick is coming home to roost. With us." Then I
told her about the dollar and how it had been lifted
from my dresser and planted on Engle. When I finished
she took a deep breath.

"My God. Anything else?"

"No. Won't that do for a while?"

"I'd say it would. But who would want to implicate
you. Why?"

"Probably it wasn't so much putting me in as it was
getting somebody out," I said dryly. I turned my wrist
up and shifted a bit until a shaft of moonlight filtering
through the tree fell on the dial. "Almost three," I said.
"And tomorrow could very well be a rough day. Shall
we?" She ground out her smoke, I stepped on mine and
we turned back toward the house. We passed a concrete
park bench set under a tree and I thought Kate slowed
a little. When we came to the next one she stopped.

"Maybe we'd better get aquainted all over again,
Marty. I'm trying to figure you out."

"I'll help," I smiled. "I know the subject thoroughly."
She sat down on the park bench and tilted her head

back, her long yellow hair touching the trunk of a jacaranda tree. I parked beside her and said, "Shoot."

"Not a bad idea."

"What? What's eating you, kiddo? Change your mind?"

"No. Let's forget that for a while. Let's talk about
you—and money."

"That won't take long. I haven't enough to run the
conversation past one short breath."

She shook her head. "There it is again." She straightened up and turned toward me, her hand resting lightly
on my arm. "Does everyone with a ten-dollar bill come
under the heading of idle rich, Marty?" I frowned and
she went on. "Maybe it's the car. Or an estate like this
or—or a yacht, but there's something. Something big
that you want pretty bad, Marty, and can't have. So
everything you see is put in terms of what it cost. I—
wish you wouldn't do that."

I didn't say anything and the next thing I knew a
warm hand was creeping into mine. I tightened my fingers over hers and said, "For instance?"

"For instance 'seven thousand dollars worth of chrome
and gray leather', Marty. Do you resent my owning that
car?"

"Hell, no. It was just a remark, Kate."

"Sure. But it practically shouts your feelings."

"One crack. One mention of money and—"

"There have been others."

"Name one."

"Well, this afternoon Mrs. Pilcher was, as far as you
were concerned, a pudgy character with a forty-dollar
swim suit and a fifty-dollar corset. And before that there
was the air-conditioning unit in my car. To me it's an
appliance that cools the air; to you it was six hundred
dollars. Why, Marty?"

She was right, of course. Looking back I could see
I'd been stacking everything up against the pile of green-

backs it would take to buy it. I scraped around for an answer, and then I felt her other hand getting into the act. Soft fingers tracing the back of my hand holding hers.

"Maybe it's the pool," I said slowly, "and the fact that I never seem to get any closer to building one as the days roll past."

"Like Engle's?"

"No. No, a commercial venture, Kate." And then I told her about how I'd planned to set it up some day. She listened and I talked about drainage and locker facilities and a bar with a sliding front that would close it off while the youngsters were splashing around during the day but which would be a very cozy feature indeed for party rental in the evening. It was almost three-thirty when I looked at my watch and we started back toward the house.

"So you can see it'll take a lot of capital," I said. "A sizable investment. It's going to take Marty Bowman a long time to lay it away on a lifeguard's pay."

"There's always the bank, Marty. Have you tried any of them?"

"No," I said, and gave her a wry smile. "I've got sixty thousand stashed away in my account all right, only I've forgotten which bank it's in. Silly of me, wasn't it, but that's how careless we rich people get with our dough."

She shook her head. "Maybe I was wrong. Maybe you've been in the sun too long."

We came through the row of trees bordering the plunge. The pool was almost full now, and when I bent to scoop a handful of water it was quite warm. We walked in silence up to the house and around the back walk along the side toward the hill. At Kate's door we stopped.

Our eyes met and she disengaged her hand, whispered

a hasty good night, and was gone.

I slipped into my own place with as little noise as I could, washed my face, undressed and sat down on the bed. One thing—I felt a hell of a lot better being on the level for a change. And it would have been damned embarrassing to Kate if it came out that she'd hired a detective to investigate her host. Now there was a chance to hide that whole side of the picture, keep it all from coming to light. I smoked in silence until the hands of the clock pointed four, then put on a robe, and went quietly through the house to the snack bar. I drew a cup of coffee and sat down to listen. Not a sound. I lifted the receiver of the telephone and heard the reassuring buzz in my ear. Then I dialed long distance and put in a call to my own place in Santa Monica.

"I'll ring you back," the operator said cheerfully.

"No, thanks. I'll just hang on," I said. I didn't want the bell on this end to arouse anyone. After several minutes I heard the rhythmic muffled sound as the local operator on the other end plugged in my phone, and then a sleepy hello came over the wire.

Seven

"FRED? MARTY." I said, my lips close to the mouthpiece "Come out of it, boy. There have been developments."

"Oh?" I heard him stifle a comfortable yawn. "Whatsamatter?"

I didn't want to stay on the phone all night and knowing Fred I decided that the first thing was to get him awake. "The gent who owns that estate the blonde and I are visiting is dead. Murdered, I think, or at least it looks that way. And dumped into the plunge."

"What the hell, Marty! You guys up there haven't been passing the punch bowl too often, have—" He broke off and I guessed he was finally all the way out of the fog. "Good Christ. What in hell happened?"

"It hasn't changed any since I just told you," I reminded him softly. "Engle—George Engle, the guy who pays the bill on this layout—is no longer with us. Since midnight. And you haven't heard the half."

"I'll brace myself, kid. Turn it loose."

I did. Talking with my face halfway down in the mouthpiece, I gave him the scoop, and it took a while. I got it all the way down to the dollar and what happened to that. "So can they get prints off of money that's been in the water, Fred?" I wanted to know.

"If you were on that buck at all clearly and no one rubbed it off, you're still there, Marty."

"And Toland will know it."

"He will. As soon as he gets a report. And won't that be a pretty kettle of tuna. I'd better get in touch with Gregory. There's going to be a lovely smell when this one gets on the breeze. Him sending out an unlicensed operator and all. Cripes!"

"We might be able to hold that part in," I reminded him.

"For the love of God, try."

"For sure, Fred. But in the meantime, how about turning the wheels at your end. I'll give you the names of all five of the guests. With Sandy Engle, his wife, that makes it an even half dozen. And you'd better not waste any time because when Toland begins to put all the pieces in place he's going to star me in the lineup."

"It doesn't look good," Fred agreed.

"You can play that record over," I said. "Hell, if I was Toland I'd be sweeping out a cell for Bowman before breakfast."

Fred wrote down the names and said he'd see what

could be done. I hung up, poured my cold coffee down the sink, washed the cup, put it away, and started to leave. As I went through the door something caught my eye. A cigarette butt near the door jamb. I bent down to look. It had a faint pink color, just a hint of lipstick as though the woman had already wiped off her make-up in preparation for bed, but enough remained to make a slight stain. When I touched the flat brown end where someone's shoe had stamped the butt out, the tobacco was still warm.

Back in the darkness of my room I smoked and tried to decide who had been listening. At first it seemed that if Kate had come down she would have waited until I was through and maybe passed a few minutes. But I had given her name to Fred. She wouldn't particularly have enjoyed that part of our little conversation. And of course it could have been Sandy Engle, Mrs. P, or the babe with the smooth henna job. I puzzled over it for a few more drags, then ground out the ember and dropped off from the sheer weight of nervous exhaustion.

It seemed I'd no more than crawled across the bed when the knock came. I rubbed sleep out of my eyes with the backs of my hands and sat up, then swung my feet over the side and felt around for slippers.

The knock came again, strong and loud, and just a little official. "Yeah, be with you in a second," I called. I pulled on a pair of slacks and opened the door. Toland's boy Widdle gave me a stern look, then stepped into the room.

"Mr. Toland wants to see you. Right away. In the living room, Mr. Bowman."

"Sure. I'll be with you as soon as I brush my teeth and comb my hair."

"I'll wait."

I turned back for a closer look, got a cool once-over from the second in command, and went toward the bathroom. Cold water splashed into the bowl. I dunked both hands under the stream of water and brought its cooling freshness to my face and neck, then squeezed an inch of toothpaste onto the brush and polished the ivories.

"What's the occasion, Widdle?" I called through the open door.

"Sheriff will tell you. Let's hurry it up, please."

I rinsed away the toothpaste and grinned at the face in the mirror. If our boy Toland had ants in his pants already this morning I might not get another chance at the razor for quite a while. I voted myself time for a shave. Then I thought about the possibilities of my ending up in the *bastille* before this day was over and it seemed like a good idea to add a bath. I swung the glass door and flipped the shower handle.

"Come on, Bowman. Let's go," Widdle complained. "I could have been down there by now."

"It takes me longer," I said. "I wash." He came and stood at the bathroom door while I shucked out of pants, shorts and slippers and stepped under the spray. Ten minutes later I got into fresh clothes and followed Bob Widdle toward the living room. My coming made the turnout a hundred per cent. Toland got up when Widdle and I entered and motioned me into a chair.

"Just taking a little concensus here, Bowman," the sheriff said easily, "on this and that. For instance, this heart ailment of Engle's. Some seem to have known about it, others didn't. Did you?"

"No. I believe I explained that I was here as a friend of one of the guests. I didn't take his blood pressure."

"Keep your shirt on, Bowman." His look might have meant anything. "So far we've established that only the doctor here knew. You others haven't heard it mentioned. Not even casually, sort of. No one—not even you, Mrs. Engle?"

He looked around and no one said anything. Toland's

thick fingers scratched the side of his face as his eyes went from person to person.

"You keep forgetting the autopsy," I pointed out. "Won't a bad ticker show up?"

"They're working—" Toland broke off with a quick glance at Sandy Engle. "We'll have that report directly," he said, "but I thought I'd just see which of Engle's friends he'd confided in. Know why? Because I had my office girl get on the phone early this morning and contact the doctors in Newhall. Not too many, you see, and she finally ran down a doc who's given Engle about three exams in the last two years. Engle was a health addict, it seems. Dieting for his waistline and all—regular check-up every six months. A Dr. Crandy was his favorite. And you know something? That secret about Engle's heart ailment was pretty well kept. Doc Crandy wasn't in on it either."

Pilcher's jaw dropped open. "You mean—"

"Exactly, gentlemen. If your Mr. Engle had a bad pump it got past his present doctor. Which leaves us with a problem, Dr. Cronk. Maybe this would be a good time for a few words from you. They'd make right interesting listening."

Cronk cleared his throat. "Actually, Sheriff, it isn't ethical for me to discuss Dr. Crandy's qualifications—" He stood up and began to pace nervously across in front of the empty fireplace. "You see, I—"

"Yes?" Toland prompted softly.

"Well, there's more here than the heart ailment itself. That is—"

He broke off again, but this time it was a legitimate stall. The Philippino had appeared and now nodded toward the sheriff. "A phone call, sir. This way, please."

Toland scratched the side of his face again, then turned to follow the servant. At the door he stopped.

"While I'm gone, doctor, maybe you could boil your

discussion down a little and get it to where we can make some sense out of it. So far you haven't said a thing. Not a thing."

Toland left with a severe look all the way around. Cronk collapsed on an overstuffed and stared moodily toward the blackened bricks of the hearth. I went over to Kate who was holding down one end of the huge leather lounge and parked beside her.

"How'd you sleep, kitten?"

"Don't joke, Marty. This looks serious. I'm thinking about what you said last night—" She lowered her voice and added—"about Dr. Cronk. His really being a physician, I mean."

"And so?"

"He's hedging a little. I'm wondering if maybe you weren't right. He just doesn't sound competent."

I patted her hand and waited. When Toland came back he had definitely heard some kind of word on Engle and it could have been important. Toland's weathered face had the expression you find on a poker player who's filled up a full house and is overdoing the dead-pan act.

"And now, Dr. Cronk?"

"I have decided to give you the facts, Sheriff," Cronk said slowly. "There doesn't seem to be any good reason for holding back any longer. I have made a great effort to spare this little lady additional pain." Here Cronk nodded sadly toward Sandy Engle, let his eyes fall to the carpet, and went on. "It was almost midnight when I heard the shout from the direction of the pool. I—we hurried down there, all of us arriving at about the same time, you might say. This fellow Bowman was bent over Engle. Naturally, being a doctor, I was called upon to render assistance, but as soon as I felt for a pulse I knew that George was dead. Now—George Engle was a strong swimmer. One of the best, considering his age, and kneeling there with my hand on his wrist, I—well,

I felt that something was wrong—that it wasn't really an accidental drowning."

"Uh-huh," Toland said softly. He fingered his pencil and shot a quick look my way, then turned back to Cronk. I felt Kate's hand tighten on mine and guessed that she had figured out what was coming. Marty Bowman was about to get the shaft.

"You knew something was wrong," Toland prompted. "And then?"

"It seemed best not to excite anyone more than they already were," Cronk said slowly. "Mrs. Engle was beside George and one could hardly add to her distress by shouting that he had been murdered. You can see that, Sheriff."

"Go on, Doctor." ˎ

"So I fell back on the quickest thing which came to mind. The heart. I simply announced that Engle had either died of a heart ailment or suffered an attack while swimming and drowned. Any other way of handling the situation would have warned the guilty person, perhaps even given him time to escape."

"Just a second—" Widdle broke in, but Dr. Cronk held up his hand and smiled a knowing smile. Just the same, he was sweating a little.

"Your young assistant is about to point out that there has been ample time to give you the truth, Sheriff, since last night. True, and I regret that I didn't do exactly that. But may I go on please?"

"Go ahead," Toland said grimly.

"Very well. Now as I said, we were all standing there and I had just announced the probable cause of George Engle's death. I had mentioned that I would handle the death certificate, in order not to distress Mrs. Engle further, or to alarm the guilty person. I planned to slip to the phone later and call you quietly. In the meantime I tried to get Bowman to stop tampering with the body.

"But he refused. In the face of a physician's pronouncement that Engle was dead, Mr. Bowman insisted on pushing and pulling on Engle right up until the moment you arrived. It was quite obvious, Sheriff, that his ardent attempt at resuscitation had a reason."

"And the reason?" Toland asked.

Cronk talked on, his voice low and persuasive, and flavored with just the right touch of professional and impersonal recounting of a situation. I closed my eyes and listened to him tell Sheriff Toland that I worked over Engle a good forty minutes—actually to obliterate any possible clues connecting me to the killing.

"You couldn't persuade Bowman to stop, Doctor?"

"I tried, but he was adamant. It was that and one other thing Bowman did which made me more angry than a man should get. Bowman insisted on my calling you. It was sort of adding insult to injury, Sheriff. The man was so secure in his belief that no one would see through his little scheme that he actually wanted the sheriff's office to be notified. And it led me into a grave mistake, I fear. There is, in all of us, a rather strong urge to dabble in crime. Most of us think that, given an opportunity, we'd make pretty good detectives, and I must confess that for a few hours after Engle's death I was so infuriated by Bowman's cocksure attitude that I was determined to see what he would do next to incriminate himself further. I realize now it was a silly thing to do, and I certainly apologize to you if I've lost you time. But I was hoping to nail him for you myself."

"I'm flattered you've decided to trust us, Doctor." Toland grunted. "But maybe not quite sold. I'd like to see a few more sides to this piece before I decide on the shape of things."

And then the redhead got into the game on my side, and as far as I was concerned, she was welcome. "I should certainly hope so, Sheriff," she said firmly. "There are six people who could have taken a hand in this—seven from your point of view, because while I know I'm not involved, you don't—and how can you make any kind of decision on the word of one of us?"

"How, indeed," I echoed, "and thanks, Elsa."

"One at a time," Toland said sharply. "What exactly is your point, young lady?"

"Simply that if the doctor wasn't sincere when he offered to handle things without calling the police, then he's missed his chance at a fortune. Hollywood can use men who read lines with the conviction Dr. Cronk put into his words last night."

Cronk bounced back with a genial, "A starlet who doubles as a talent scout? Easy, young lady. You can see what a mess I got into just by trying to do another man's job."

Elsa gave him a long level treatment with steady brown eyes, then turned back to the sheriff. "I'd like to hear Mr. Bowman's side of this," she said evenly.

"Sure." Toland grinned. "We'll hear everyone's side. Maybe more than once. How about it, young man?"

I wet my lips and tried to frame the words. Where did I start? My silver dollar might be one place to tee off, but Fred had said those prints would show only if I had left a nice clear set. I wasn't sure about that; I'd tossed the thing a time or two. It could be that Engle's fingers had rubbed the coin clear of any I may have left. And hitting back at Cronk seemed hardly worth while. He had made quite a case against me, but he'd kept it on an impersonal plane for the most part and bickering wouldn't help.

Or would it? I turned toward Cronk. "For one thing, Doctor, we might start with your brief diagnosis last night. Brief? It was practically non-existent. Mind telling us what kind of doctor you are?"

"My professional procedure isn't subject to your approval, Bowman." Cronk said stiffly. "I happen to be a radiologist."

"Then you're not really a doctor of medicine at all."

"A radiologist is like an eye specialist or an obstetrician or any other specialist. We all receive general training and despite my specialty, I'm an M.D. The sheriff can check if he likes."

"We checked," Toland said. "An office and X-ray lab. San Diego. We sent a wire. In fact everyone here seems to be pretty much what he said he was last night. We've been burning up the phone and all, and the autopsy report just came a while ago." He paused, then went on, "There was, of course, no evidence of heart trouble. Engle was as sound as a fence-post."

"Then he did drown?" I asked.

"No, son, he was dead going into the pool. They didn't find water in him. None at all, and while there's never a whole lot, there's always a little when a guy goes out that way. So, now we can eliminate the women. George Engle was strangled, or otherwise suffocated, maybe with a beach towel or some such thing, and pushed into the pool. He wasn't a kid any more, but I can't see how any of these girls could have turned the trick."

He finished with a careful look at his now shortened list of possible candidates for the deep breathing exercises at San Quentin: Pilcher, Doc Cronk, and Marty Bowman.

Eight

TOLAND'S WEATHER-BEATEN FACE was turned toward me, his steady gray eyes asking a silent question. Doc Cronk had managed very nicely in the short interval that Toland had been away to the phone. I felt I could use a break myself.

I forced a smile. "If it's all the same to you, Sheriff, I'd like to down a bit of breakfast before starting this one. It could, you know, turn out to be a long session."

"Couldn't it?" Mrs. Pilcher said sourly. "And for some more than others."

I didn't see any point in getting into an argument with Pilcher's fat wife. I turned back to the sheriff.

"Fact is," he said, "we're all having a bite. On the terrace, I think she said. That right, Mrs. Engle?"

Sandy nodded, tight-lipped, got up and went through the door leading toward the kitchen. When she came back she said, "They're starting to bring it out now. If any of you care to freshen up—"

She let it trail off and the warring clans drew apart. I watched Pilcher and his wife go toward their room, then Cronk left. Toland nodded to Widdle and the pair of them went out onto the terrace. When I took Kate's arm and piloted her through the glass doors leading toward the terrace and pool, Elsa Doyle fell in beside us and matched our steps.

"Thanks for your help, Miss Doyle," I said. "It's appreciated."

"Elsa," she said with a smile. I murmured that my name was Marty and Kate tossed her first name into the hat. She drew a very warm and friendly smile from the redhead.

Elsa said, "That Cronk! After the quick way he wanted to give up on any attempt to save George last night—and now he really has you in trouble with Toland, I'm afraid."

I gave her a short nod. She was worth thinking about—she'd spoken to me but looked at Kate. Why? Because Elsa Doyle had an eighteen-carat mind under that carefully done red hair. It was obvious to all that Kate and I were together up here at Engle's and Elsa wasn't risking friction in that direction. She was being friendly to our cause, just a shade distant with me, and glowingly warm with Kate. It was a technique calculated to make her friends where it mattered.

The three of us found a round metal table, complete with striped umbrella overhead, and when the Philippino rolled out his little portable buffet we went over, lined up for bacon, scrambled eggs, orange juice and coffee, and carried our loot back to the poolside.

For the next half hour I said "Yes," and "No," and "It would seem you might have something there," in the right places but quietly I was trying to evaluate my latest position and what could be done about it. If Kate had really leveled with me on the reasons for my being here, a vague picture of the Engle setup was taking shape. It wasn't pretty. And I would have trouble proving it.

For one thing, I couldn't explain that I'd been asked to investigate the Engle estate. Boreland Gregory would be out on a limb and so would Kate. But I thought I could put the squeeze on Cronk, and I figured to give it a try. I could point up plenty of inconsistencies in his story and intended to have the Doc explain a few of them. It would keep him busy for a while at least, keep him from tightening the net on Marty Bowman.

Then there was Dan Pilcher. Both he and his wife had added their weight against me. There had to be a reason for that. It would only be natural that anyone helping G.E. into the great beyond would be most anxious to have a good candidate for the scapegoat. Which led me to the redhead again. She was trying to get me out of this and as far as I was concerned, it let her out from under, at least for the time being. Finally I brought Sandy Engle under consideration. Knocking off a hubby isn't exactly unknown in these parts, and if you don't go along with Toland's quick dismissal of the women present, Sandy would certainly have to be weighed a time or two. I still had her on the scales when Toland and Bob Widdle sauntered over, followed by the overweight threesome. Toland sent Widdle for Mrs. Engle, then turned to me.

"Now last night you had Mr. Engle face down on the grass, Bowman, just about there." He pointed with his thick forefinger to the spot where Engle had lain. "You were giving him artificial respiration when I got here. We'll have to admit that the doctor has fairly well explained his part, so—"

"That isn't quite unanimous, Sheriff," I objected. "He's built up a case against me, but I'm afraid it's a trifle thin in places."

"You could point out those spots if you would, Bowman," Toland invited. He turned around to nod to Sandy who had just arrived, then raised a questioning eyebrow in my direction.

"Well, for one thing, Dr. Cronk's decision that Engle was beyond help came too damn fast, Sheriff. He barely touched Engle's face and pronounced the man dead." I shook my head. "Maybe he had a finger on George's wrist, maybe not. In any event he didn't move it enough to open the hand. You found a coin there, you said."

"He's a doctor, Bowman."

"A radiologist. An X-ray man," I corrected.

"I have explained," Cronk cut in, "that I am an M.D.— a full-fledged member of the medical profession, Bowman, but specializing in X-ray."

"Then you should be well aware that a drowned person's pulse is often too weak to be found in the wrist. Any honest-to-john medic ought to know that."

"But it turns out Engle didn't drown," Cronk countered.

"Maybe *you* knew that at the time," I grinned, "but the rest of us didn't. At least I didn't—hence the effort to start his breathing. An effort to which you offered about every objection in the book. Remember?"

"You're twisting mv words, Bowman," Cronk said sharply. He was getting a little excited. Fair enough. He couldn't get too hot under the collar for me. I poured on the fuel.

"The sheriff didn't tell us George hadn't drowned until today. Care to find a good reason why you knew it last night?"

"Now just a moment, Bowman. As a member of the medical profession, I judged Engle dead. I have explained why I gave a false reason, but the man was past help and I said so. It was obvious to me."

"Once again, how was it obvious?" I asked softly. I was getting ready to dive into some pretty shallow water, but there wasn't any other way.

"Bowman!" Cronk stormed. "In my professional opinion George had already died when I was summoned. The pulse. Other factors too, and I am getting a little weary of your questioning my decision in that matter. As a doctor—"

"Stop kidding," I cut in quickly. "You aren't a doctor. You wouldn't know a broken leg from the pink-eye."

Cronk caught his breath and you could have heard a leaf drop in Engle's pool. Toland looked at me as if I'd just said something unholy and righteous indignation was beginning to build in Bob Widdle's face.

"We've checked that, Bowman," Widdle said severely. "You'll remember that the sheriff mentioned it this morning."

"You found he had a practice. You didn't check his credentials."

"Just a minute, Bowman," Cronk raged, his face getting about three shades farther into the red. "That last statement was as close to libel as I care to hear you come."

"Now, men," Toland said soothingly, "we'll have to calm down a mite here. We aren't going to get anyplace this way."

"Don't bet on that, Sheriff." I grinned. "Last night Cronk had never heard of McBurney's point. Any doctor is as familiar with that as he is with the steering wheel of his car. And there are other things. Things he didn't do for Engle that any doctor would have done."

"Bowman, I'll—"

"Go ahead and sue," I said, and tried to sound like a man with confidence.

"No. No, the sheriff is right. It isn't going to help any for us to get excited. You're a little overwrought, Bowman, and the least I can do is overlook—"

"Go on," I grinned. "Be nasty. Be as nasty as Marty Bowman and sue the pants off him."

Cronk fumbled for a handkerchief. He gave careful attention to wiping his glasses while regrouping his forces. When he slipped the specs in place he turned to Toland.

"Go ahead with your work, Sheriff," he said. "There isn't any point in my complicating things at the moment with a personal side issue. I shall deal with Mr. Bowman through the courts when we've finished with this unfortunate situation."

Now I was sure. He managed to keep the voice steady but his lips trembled and his eyes were careful to avoid mine. I'd gambled and won, and I felt a vast relief. I could grind right into him now, but I saw a doubt working into Toland's face and it would be much more effective if he did the honors. I'd slipped the knife into Cronk. Now I could rest a while and let the sheriff twist the blade a little. When he turned toward me and asked what in hell McBurney's point had to do with what, I silently jerked my thumb toward Cronk.

"Well?" Toland asked. "What's it all about, Doctor?"

Cronk eyed me speculatively and gave it one more

try. "You've got me, Sheriff," he said, his voice holding that nervous edge. "I think Bowman should see a psychiatrist. He's slipping over the edge."

"Uh-huh," Toland said heavily. "Me, I don't know which one of you two is tilted, but I'll sure as hell find out. Bob, you wanna sit here and sun yourself while we have a short breather? I'm going to get on that phone and see what's what. Hell's bells, maybe I'm the one that's losing his marbles."

I bent down at the edge of the pool and dipped a hand into the warm water, then snapped my fingers a few times, and when the dry desert air spirited away the last of the moisture, I found my smokes. I passed the pack to Kate and Elsa and offered one to Sandy but she shook her head.

"Bright boy," Kate said. She favored me with a look that made me feel good all over.

"Lucky shot," I grinned, and struck two matches at once. Three lights from the pair of matches, and we settled back to enjoy cigarettes. "He looks bad," I said, and nodded in the general direction of Doc Cronk.

"And sad," Elsa said lightly. "Do you notice a slight cooling off on the part of the other couple?"

I nodded. Pilcher and his wife had drawn a few feet away from the doctor and were holding one of those casual, low-toned discussions that aren't casual at all. First one would speak, then I'd see the lips of the other take over, and the strain on both of their faces told me they were more than a little worried. Like a pair of two-bit city employees who might have backed the wrong candidate in a local election. I enjoyed their misery for something like five minutes and then Frank Toland walked heavily toward us. Cronk looked up, his pan wearing all of the hope-against-hope you'd expect to see on the face of a man in the death cell.

"Well?" he said.

"I put it to Dr. Crandy," Toland said grimly. "I asked him if he knew anything about McBurney's point—where it was. He laughed and said naturally he did. So then I asked what he'd think of a doctor who didn't know." Toland fixed an accusing eye on Cronk. "Crandy said he'd probably think the same thing about that doctor that I'd think about a sheriff who didn't know what a pair of handcuffs were."

Toland pulled his wide-brimmed hat off and touched his sleeve to his forehead, then settled the hat in place. "It turns out that this McBurney's point is on the stomach, Cronk, and anybody goes to an M.D. about a belly-ache, they start working around this place to see if maybe his appendix is kicking up a fuss. Very common. One of the first steps a doctor takes, Crandy says. I'm afraid we'll have to award that round to Bowman. You have the floor, Cronk."

Cronk looked toward the sheriff, then dropped his head and stared at the grass under his feet. When he spoke his voice was halting and low and utterly defeated.

"Sure. I guess that's the end of it. You'd check and you'd find out. I'm practicing under a false certificate—a diploma mill job. Radiology I can handle—have handled for quite a while. I worked as a technician, and then in the Army X-ray lab. Enough years to learn all that was necessary—" His face showed how hard this was for him to say, and under other circumstances I might almost have felt sorry for him. Suddenly he burst out, "But don't think I'm the only one up here that's under Engle's thumb. Or was. They're all in the same boat, Sheriff. Every one of them. I'm not standing for this one alone. I didn't kill him. I didn't, and I don't know who did, but I do know one thing. Pilcher—the movie girl—everyone, they all were buying insurance from George Engle."

"Insurance. Well, that was his business," Toland said. "You haven't helped us any there."

"We had to buy it, Sheriff, all of us. Premiums paid in cash—no checks accepted. Which sounds good, only you pay and pay and pay and you never mentioned to George that he hadn't ever gotten around to making out a policy."

Nine

KATE DREW a quick breath and I heard Pilcher swearing softly. Elsa Doyle stood looking from the doc to me, then to the sheriff and back to me again.

"This Bowman," she said in a low voice. "He's a pretty sharp beach boy." She gave me an admiring look that could have matched the ones you get from a teen-ager you've just lugged out of a rip tide. I scrambled around for a quick change in subject.

"Just one of those things," I said. "Something left over from an appendix operation I had as a kid. But didn't he say we were all in the same life raft? I seem to remember that you got special mention along with pudgy pants over there."

Elsa Doyle laughed. "That Cronk. He's in such a stew right now he'd probably say that the sheriff was under George's thumb too. I'm going to wait for a great deal more in the way of evidence before I start thinking that you people are out on the blackmail limb."

"Thanks," Kate said, and matched the redhead's laugh. "If we believe everything we hear we'll be sleeping with the bureau drawers propped against the door."

"Did you say—blackmail?"

We turned. Sandy Engle was standing there. She looked from one to another, then put an unsteady hand on the back of a deck chair and faced Cronk. "Do you mean my husband was blackmailing you?"

"That's exactly what Dr. Cronk has implied," Toland said grimly. "And Cronk further indicates that the rest of the inmates of this fun house are in the same fix. Just how much do you know about this, Mrs. Engle? Maybe you can help us a little."

"But George couldn't have. He's such a—so—" She broke it there and big tears formed in her eyes. "I can't believe that George—" Once again she let it trail off, then turned and ran blindly toward the house. Kate Weston hurried after her, slipped an arm around her waist, and the heavy outer door closed after them. Sheriff Toland sat down on the edge of a patio lounge and raised a questioning eyebrow at Cronk.

"Let's have it, Cronk. You're under a false flag. How did you get there, fella, and all about it. I'd like to get things straight."

Cronk tugged at the belt circling his ample middle and then adjusted his glasses. Out of the corner of my eye I saw Mrs. Pilcher giving her husband a nervous glance as Cronk dropped wearily into a canvas chair.

"I'm willing to go into this, Toland," Cronk said dejectedly, "but remember that I've told you I'm not alone. I'm not going to hang for something I didn't do, by God. Not when there's a half a dozen other people with just as much motive and a hell of a lot more chance to finish George off. He keeps an office and collects his money, but that's the only way you could consider him a business man. He had plenty on all of us. And a few other people, I'd guess. Like me—like knowing I wasn't really an M.D."

"He knew you when?" Toland asked.

"No, he didn't. Nobody here in California did, until four years ago."

Cronk's head slumped a little lower as he went on, his voice almost listless as he told us how he'd been a shoe clerk in a small Illinois town before the war. About ten thousand population, Cronk said, a handful of doctors and a single X-ray lab. The lab was next door to the store in which Cronk spent his working day fitting size ten feet with size nine shoes which he cheerfully sold as size seven and a half. People, he was beginning to find, were very gullible indeed.

But each year in the shoestore seemed to advance him only slightly along the path to financial success. His salary went up slowly and was highly dependent on the labor market. He laid by very little from the world's store of luxury, and more and more he came to envy the owner of that lab next to the shoestore. No midnight hours. No calls in the dark of night to break his sleep. An honest M.D., sure, but he had an ideal practice. He did the X-ray work for the other doctors in town. An assistant, quickly trained and not too hard on the budget handled the actual equipment. The doctor read the plates and wrote out his report.

Through dint of some study and with the cooperation of his medico neighbor, Cronk changed trades. He came cheaper than the trained technician the doc already had, and who was ready to move to greener pastures. Albert Cronk learned as he worked—and the Army put on the finishing touches. Through basic, Cronk put in for and received a transfer to a hospital unit. Working day and night, he pursued his chores with a diligence rare among Uncle Sam's temporary help and wangled his way into the X-ray lab of a moderately large base.

And here he managed to stay. Two years of: "Take a deep breath, hold it—now breathe—" as countless dog-faces stood for their chest X-rays. Then on to the gastro-intestinal wards and a liberal education in fluoroscopes.

Each week he added to his store of information, kept notes and labored to learn the routines. He studied reports made out on hundreds of plates and after hours slipped as many of them as time would allow against the illuminated ground glass and carefully traced the irregularities as he read reports. In short, he apprenticed himself to the trade. Realizing that disposition of the cases was left largely to attending physicians and that the radiologist did little more than interpret the X-rays, Cronk poured his entire accumulation of spare time into that channel.

Now, sitting beside Engle's pool, Cronk seemed more than a little proud of the skill he had attained without formal training.

"Your service time comes to over four years, then. That right, Cronk?" Toland asked.

"Almost five," Cronk said. "Toward the end I used to hold the plates up to a light before stacking them in the racks for the doctors. I'd make out a report on each one or as many as I had time for—write it all out in a notebook I kept with me. Then after the X-ray had been analyzed by the doc I'd check myself. You know—go in and read his analysis and see how far I'd missed on each one. And you'd be amazed at the accuracy I attained. I'm not going to apologize for the cash I took in since then, Sheriff. I can read an X-ray with the best of them. I've seen a lot more plates than plenty of the practicing radiologists who've spent all that time in medical school."

"The medical association is going to take a dim view of your logic," Toland said dryly. "What about your credentials?"

"A diploma mill, as I said."

"Where, Cronk?"

Cronk looked at his shoes. "Kansas City—I think. I'm not exactly sure I can help you on that."

"You could try. What was the name of the man who set you up in business? How did you meet him?"

"It's a little hazy, Toland. Like an abortionist—did

you know some of them actually advertise in the daily papers—some pass as urinologists, some as midwives—but you'd have a hell of a time pinning anything on them. They get their credentials the way I got mine—a fellow I met in the Army sent me an ad from a New York paper and—"

"Where did you go to make the deal, Cronk?"

"A hotel room in Kansas City. But that was just a meeting place. Nothing was written and I paid off with small bills totaling five hundred and fifty dollars. I started in the outskirts of a middle-sized town in the East—had letterheads printed and all, then moved to San Diego and used my short stay in the East as a reference point. You'd be surprised how much credence people are inclined to place in easily obtainable props, such as business cards, letterhead correspondence, and the rest."

Toland scratched a hard finger along his jaw and gave Cronk a careful once-over. "It hardly seems possible that you could get by with the work, though. I mean there'd be times when you didn't know—"

Cronk almost managed a wry grin. "You'd be surprised, Sheriff, what goes on. Men by the hundred are hired as machinists in your town, for instance, then put to work on some simple routine operation that a high school kid could learn to do in three days. The machinist is trained but he doesn't have to use more than an infinitesimal part of that skill. Now you take my work. A chest X-ray I can read. As well as any man in the business, I'd venture. You look for scar tissue, active spots—a few other things. As a 'doctor,' too, other doctors are available to you for consultation. Then suppose a man is sent in to have a picture of his arm taken. Simple. The technician exposes a few plates. Then you find the breaks or cracks if any, which are actually quite obvious on the plate, dash off a short note, and send the works along to the fellow's physician. *You* don't have to set the bone. Or advise how it's to be done. You're through when you've made the picture and pointed out the break."

Toland sighed heavily. "So you were doing all right, then, until—"

"Until about four years ago, as I said. In the Army I'd been careful to make damn few friends. I kept my head down, hid myself away among the many, but of course there's a limit on how far you can go with that, too. I did figure, though, when I set up in practice, that the chances were almost nil that I'd ever encounter anyone who knew me sufficiently well to recall that I'd been a mere technician. Even among those, very few would guess my actual background. But luck was against me, and one day I had to X-ray a fellow named Gorton sent over by one of the neighborhood doctors. This Gorton, he'd been a corpsman on the base I worked last. One of these sharpies, and naturally I told him I'd worked through medical school after the war but he got around to reading my diploma on the wall and the date was 1946. He grinned and said it looked like I'd hung up some kind of a record—out of the army as an enlisted technician in late '45 and a graduate M.D. the next year. I couldn't kid him out of it.

"A few days later he came around and wanted to borrow some money. Two hundred bucks, he said. I took one long look at the possibilities and decided not to go for it. He got sore, but not too sore and I figured he'd think it over and forget it. To be quite honest, I knew Gorton pretty well. He wasn't what you'd call a man of guts and blackmail takes a certain amount of courage. But if I guessed right on Gorton's being afraid to embark on outright blackmail I missed on what he'd do about it, because about a month later George Engle drove down from L.A. to pay me a visit."

"Now just a second," Widdle cut in. "You were talking about a guy named Gorton. How did Engle get into this?"

Cronk gave Widdle an annoyed glance, then turned back to Sheriff Toland. "As you may have gathered from the unhappy faces around here in the last half hour, George Engle spread his operation over quite a wide and lucrative area. He—" Cronk hesitated a moment and blotted perspiration from his forehead, then adjusted his glasses and went on. "There's one in every city, I guess. Hard, shrewd and ruthless. Sure, he didn't seem that way. Not here, treating us all as guests and the like, but you don't know Engle." Cronk stopped again as Kate came down the walk and sat down beside me.

"How's Mrs. Engle?" Toland asked.

"She's pretty broken up—wants to be alone for a while, she said. I thought it might be best too, because she's embarrassed to death. She had no idea, I'm sure, that George wasn't a legitimate insurance broker. It was something of a shock."

"I can guess," I said seriously. Looking toward Dan Pilcher I saw a sardonic sneer working its way across his fat face. He raised a chubby hand long enough to remove the ever-present toothpick.

"A hell of a bad guess, Bowman. You ask me, I'd say she knew her husband pretty well."

"You mean you think she knew what George had on you, Pilcher?" I grinned.

"I didn't say that. In fact, Cronk is speaking strictly for himself, as far as I'm concerned. I'm just here as a guest—knew George personally. We were good friends."

"You're a little disorganized," I said quickly. "Make up your mind, fella, on just where you stand. A while ago you and the doc here were closer than two boys in a bathtub "

"How'd I know he was a phony?" Pilcher complained.

That earned him a sour look from Cronk and then Sheriff Toland stepped in.

"Hold on now. We aren't getting anywhere wrangling. You gents leave the questions to me for a while. We were working around to how Engle muscled in on some information a guy named Gorton happened to run onto. How about it, Cronk?"

"It's like this, Sheriff," Cronk said in a tired voice, "Everyone knows about things that are going on that aren't exactly legal. Think for a minute and you'll see I'm right. A friend of yours is collecting part of his pay in cash and manages to overlook some of it when he files his income tax. Or a buyer gets a kickback on sales to his company. Done all the time. And how many car dealers were raking in 'over-the-ceiling' bonuses during the war years? You know about these things and maybe you gripe, but you don't do anything. You don't want to look like a heel and you wouldn't be caught dead squealing to the Bureau of Internal Revenue, say, for the reward they'll gladly pay on that friend of yours who's cutting the corners a bit too close.

"Well, George Engle built a business plowing that fertile field. He let the word get around that there was cash on the line for reliable information, and complete protection for the informer. Engle paid a small part of what the information was worth, then went to work. He evaluated what his silence should bring and that was the premium. Twice each year he'd call me. 'Doctor,' he'd say, 'been thinking about your insurance the last few days. Why not come up to the desert and discuss it this weekend?' You can be sure I didn't say no. The semi-annual premium on my policy was five hundred dollars. A cool thousand a year to keep Engle from asking that an investigation of my credentials be made. It was cash in old bills, and actually very little talk of insurance." Cronk blotted his forehead again. "Now you've got the situation, Sheriff. I've played it straight across the table. You owe it to me to dig into other people here—I didn't kill Engle and I had no more reason to than the rest of them. I could afford the tariff George skimmed off me. What was he getting from Pilcher and Bowman, and Doyle? How about that blonde next to Bowman? She's been here before, I can tell you that much."

Toland drew a big breath, then looked us over with a cool eye. Bob Widdle stood up like a man about to go to work but Toland nodded toward the chair Widdle had just vacated and he sat down again.

"We'll just take it slow and easy from here on," Toland said. He pulled off his hat, regarded its broad brim, then carefully reformed the crease in the crown. "I guess you know we'll have to turn this over to the medical association, Cronk. They can take whatever legal action they like, but while we've got the body in our possession, so to speak, we'll just hang on to you until we iron out this Engle mess. For now, though, we'll let you off the hook." Toland put his hat back on and gave it a practiced tug.

"Suppose we start with you, Bowman. You were in on the ground floor when Engle was killed. You tell us how you happened to drive up here for a weekend."

"Sure," I said. "I'm as pure as ivory, you might say. Just happened to be a friend of Miss Weston's. She, you will find, was not invited up here by George, but by his wife. They've been—"

"Now, Bowman," Toland chided gently. "The lady will speak for herself. Later. I want to know about you."

"I'm explaining it to you," I said shortly. "Are you going to do this or am I?"

"You are, son," he said, his voice unruffled. "Just keep it down to your side of the picture. We want to know where you fit up here?"

"A guest. A friend of Miss Weston."

"How much was your premium, son? What did you pay Engle—and why?"

"Does there have to be one, Sheriff?"

"It would seem that way."

"Okay," I barked, "I used to drown people in the surf. See Bowman to get rid of your unwanted wives. Two hundred bucks a head. Three for half a G, special rates for the boys who make the altar hike every other year or so. That make you happy, Toland?"

"Now, son, that won't help any. I got a world of patience but you'll wear it out fast the way you're going. You just calm down and answer my questions."

I pulled my smokes out and struck a match. "All right. I'll try, Sheriff. Only don't insist on my having been blackmailed by Engle. It just isn't the case. Sorry, but that's the way she bounces."

"If you came with Miss Weston, then, Engle didn't even know you. Not until you got here, that is."

"That's right, Sheriff."

"And you haven't been here before. Ever."

I nodded.

"Uh-huh. Some of this we'll have to check with Mrs. Engle, I guess, when she's feeling up to talking with us. But for now we'll have to accept that part of it. In the meantime, we can get a few facts from some of the others."

"Just a minute," Mrs. Pilcher cut in icily. "I'd like to point out that everything isn't quite as rosy as it sounds between Mr. Bowman and this Weston woman. For instance yesterday morning on the way up here, Dan and I stopped for coffee at a small café down the road. When we came out we saw these two sitting in that big car. They had been there quite a while, Sheriff, because I heard the tires skid when they stopped out front. But they didn't get out and come in—they just sat in the car, and when we went out to get into our own auto we saw them there. You could tell they were having a spat."

"And how do you tell a thing like that?" Toland asked mildly.

Mrs. Pilcher sniffed. "They were about as far apart as two people can get in the front seat. When I came through the door they were talking real fast. I saw them, only as soon as the door slammed they looked up and noticed us. Then they stopped arguing right away."

"Well, I don't know," Toland said uncomfortably. "It would seem that—"

But I didn't hear what the sheriff was saying. My eye had wandered toward the house and my jaw must have dropped open because smoke billowed from a brick chimney on one side of the building. That chimney would be about where the master bedroom and living quarters were. George's and Sandy's room. And it was a hell of a lot too warm for a fire in the fireplace at high noon.

And then Bob Widdle shouted, "Sheriff! Look—"

Toland was already on his feet. He broke into a dead run, the rest of us following. I took the lead halfway up the walk. The topography of the house must have made an impression on me, because moments later I was slamming my knuckles against a locked door.

"Sandy!" I yelled. "Open up! It's Marty."

Then Toland pounded down the hall, sized up the situation, backed across the narrow hallway, and lunged against the door. It buckled and gave.

Sandy Engle sat in front of the small fireplace, her face toward the blue flame leaping from the open butane valve used to start wood fires in the grate. There wouldn't be any smoke coming out of the chimney now. Because the papers she had been feeding into the flames were almost gone. I watched as Toland bent toward the bricks and tried to rake a corner of a white envelope out of the glowing ashes. When he finally pinched away the ember, all he had was a half-charred bit of paper.

Ten

TOLAND FLIPPED the valve and the sword of blue flame sputtered and died. He slipped his hard brown hand over the heavy brass poker and raked thoroughly through the red glow, but the fire had consumed all trace of whatever Sandy had fed it. A wisp of ash rose with warm air currents and disappeared up the chimney.

"You haven't helped things any," Toland told her quietly. "I guess there isn't any need to ask what went up the flue just now."

Sandy's eyes roved over the carpet underfoot but her hand indicated a disk of steel swung out from the wall across the room. "Everything. Everything from the wall safe, Mr. Toland."

I took three quick strides, mounted the chair still under the safe, and looked through the opening. "She's empty," I said.

Bob Widdle motioned me down, got up for a careful search, and added his echo. "Not a thing. It's clean."

Sheriff Toland studied Sandy Engle for several seconds, then scratched his temple and said, "You must have read some of it, Mrs. Engle, to be sure of what you were burning."

"I don't know a thing," Sandy said dully, her face still downcast. "When you said—everyone said George was living on the misery of our friends, I couldn't think of what to do. How can I face people again? Our money coming—that way. I—well, it took a while for things to clear up, but when they did I knew what had to be done. I told Kate I wanted to be alone, and as soon as she left I emptied the wall safe. There were a lot of envelopes.

Plain white envelopes, each with a name written across one corner. I glanced at three or four—enough to see that the names were of people who had been George's guests from time to time—and then I burned everything."

"Uh-huh. Now look, Mrs. Engle. A man has been murdered. Your husband. Maybe he wasn't everything you thought—but we don't know that. It would help if we knew which of those present were paying hush money to Mr. Engle—if anybody was. Dr. Cronk's made the only accusation. Let's not try to be the judge and jury on this. Nothing is grounds for killing a man. If any one of these supposed victims had gone to the law it would have ended the blackmail racket. You know that."

"I can't help you, Mr. Toland," Sandy said firmly. "I didn't open a single envelope. I only saw a name or two, just enough to know that I was getting rid of his private papers. But I didn't see any names of people here now."

"You're sure of that?"

"Yes."

She said it too loud and too fast. I caught a look on her face that said she might not be leveling with Toland and I wondered if he felt it too. He nodded slowly, his leathery face serious and thoughtful. "Tell you what— I'd like to look around a bit here. No offence, ma'm, but it wouldn't seem right if I didn't try to make sure. You could all wander back out there by the pool and wait, if you would. Bob, you go along and keep the peace and I'll run through the bureaus and such here in the room."

We went back and parked under our umberella, and waited for the big man to fumble through Sandy's things. Kate tried to soothe Sandy, but understandably Sandy wanted to be apart from us. She lay in a shaded patio swing, her face buried in the soft green pad. When she asked Widdle if she might go up to the house for a blanket against the cool breeze flowing down from the hill, he gave her a curt no, then asked Elsa Doyle to get one. I wasn't sure whether or not Sandy needed the blanket for warmth or to hide in. I could see the jerking movement of her body and every now and then the sounds of violent sobbing came from the swing. We tried conversation but it didn't quite come off. Then Elsa found a lounge and stretched out and Kate excused herself similarly. I scrounged around in my chair until I was comfortable and closed my eyes.

I didn't sleep a wink.

Probably the others didn't either. My own thoughts were coming fast and strong. I felt sure Sandy had lied about not reading any of those dossiers. She'd have been a fool to burn everything sight unseen, and she was definitely not slow-witted. If she'd hidden some of them, Toland would find 'em and maybe this would wind up the proceedings in short order. I for one hoped so. I'd been a little too close to the killing to make for comfort. If Toland didn't get his hooks into a good live suspect soon he was going to stop being so choosy and when that happened he'd settle on Bowman. Of that I was quite certain. I'd broken Cronk over the rack, of course, but there was one thing I hadn't done. I hadn't offered a single argument of my own that would rub out his case against me. No one had seen Engle after I did. No one saw me bring him out. He hadn't drowned; he'd been strangled—his air choked off and Toland had pointed out that it would have taken a reasonably strong pair of hands. And Cronk, phoney or not, had shown that my artificial respiration covered a mite too neatly all finger-prints, possible bits of hair from my arms, or anything else of mine they might have found on George Engle.

Except that damned coin.

I turned to Pilchers' side of the picture and tried to see them against the background of Engle's murder. Either one of them was definitely blackmail bait—but how to prove it to Sheriff Toland? Pilcher had the strength to have cut Engle down.

Kate? She was a good enough swimmer to suggest considerable strength. Could Kate Weston have slipped a length of light rope or soft cloth around Engle's neck? True, one of the things I had been hired to work on was now an established fact. All the guests didn't come up because they liked it. Cronk by his own admission had been forced to come. Kate had added that they were bullied into making believe they enjoyed it. On that she was batting a little lower. I hadn't noticed any great pretext at enjoyment on anyone's part. Now, watching her, I tried to recall some bit of conversation, some word from George that would have told me she was not under his protective insurance and had indeed been invited by Sandy rather than the lord of the manor. Certainly Sandy seemed to consider Kate in the same light as the others, yet Sandy Engle had just discovered, or so she would like us to believe, that her ever-loving spouse was strictly poison pen. It wouldn't make a lady feel too well, you'd guess, so she would want to be alone for a while.

Pushing it a little further, I came to Elsa Doyle and Sandy Engle herself. Assuming a girl could have swung this deal would have to put both of them in the light of possible suspects. Doyle first. I tried to turn her all around in my mind and see something besides that million-dollar frame and the deluxe henna job. A cool kid, from any angle. And she'd been around. It was a lead pipe cinch that she could have been a candidate for Engle's phony insurance. But she hadn't shown the least happiness over his exit, nor had the recent loss of the stack of damning envelopes seemingly added to her pleasure. I tried to figure why and came up with one plausible answer. You would expect a rising young starlet to be a reasonably good actress, an able person at controlling her emotions.

In any case you'd have to give her that much. And this much more—she was a hundred and ten pounds of carefully cultivated feminine charm and it would still be shining through when she was sixty-seven.

That wrenched my mental excursions to Sandy Engle. We hadn't tied off many loose ends as far as Sandy was concerned. Nothing at all on why she hadn't been away from the estate or swam seldom and then at night. Shy and retiring, she had a dark-haired loveliness that seemed natural and it suited her somehow. One of those women who seldom exert any great amount of energy. You didn't see her hurrying about in the busy hostess role. She wasn't out to drink up all the liquor in the portable bar Engle had rolled out from time to time that first day—in fact I guessed that lemonade was her forte, though there was no hint that she resented the whisky and soda pouring into other people's glasses. If anything, you could call her look a wistful one—*wish I was there.* Much too docile, too lacking in force to tighten a cord around anyone's throat, I was sure.

Then I put that apparent lack of forcefulness up against Kate's suspicion that Sandy might have been forced to remain on the estate. That same force might make her reticent—but it didn't have to keep her from murder. I was beginning to wonder if there had been an envelope with Sandra Engle written across its white surface . . . after all, George wouldn't have had to entrust her with the combination to the wall safe. She could have known just where to look for it after he was dead.

The sun was warm on my face and I grew weary of grappling with the problem. I wanted to slip into a pair of swim trunks and splash around in Engle's pool for a while but it didn't look like Widdle would go for anyone's leaving long enough to change. So instead I began to do a little mental construction on my own project—that gold mine I hoped some day to own. I let my eye measure the

Engle plunge and wondered if there was anything here
I could use when I went into business. Blue tile? No, I
guessed I wouldn't go for that. In the setup I planned a
white pool would look better and I could keep the water
sparkling and blue without any help from the tile. The
drain was extra large for speedy changing of water, the
stainless steel grille sunk into the reinforced concrete to
give maximum drainage through its bottom and sides
—this kept the pool in operation practically twenty-four
hours a day. Then. . . .

I came out of it when Sandy Engle swung her feet
down and stood up. She looked around leisurely, then
folded the blanket and tossed it on the grass, ran a slow
hand through her long black hair, and went toward the
pool. She stood there several minutes, her eyes on the
water, and I watched in silence. Then we heard the noise
of a laboring car engine winding up toward the estate. It
pulled onto the parking strip and a few minutes later
Sheriff Toland came toward us, a firm smile on his brown
face, and walking beside him was a tall woman wearing
a simple business suit.

"Miss Birch," Toland said, "from our office. I hate to
bother you, Mrs. Engle, but we have to be sure about
your not holding out an envelope or two. So if you you'd
like, Miss Weston can go along, but I want you and Miss
Birch to go up to the house for a while. She'll—" Toland
hesitated. then finished—"go through your things."

"You mean search me?" Sandy asked incredulously.

"That's about it, ma'm. It would have been very
easy for you to slip some of those things from the safe
into your dress," Toland said firmly "We don't want anyone to claim later that you had, so for your protection
Miss Birch will go with you to your room."

Toland had put it nicely, I thought, and it didn't leave
Sandy Engle much of an out. Not that she appeared to
want one. She frowned momentarily, then said, "Of

course. I'll be more than glad to cooperate. No one could be more interested in seeing justice—seeing the person who killed my husband brought to trial." Then she turned and went toward the house, Miss Birch a step behind her. Sheriff Toland nodded to Kate.

"I'd really rather you went along. Miss Birch isn't a policewoman or anything—just our one-woman office force. It might be much better if you were to sort of add a third voice to the proceedings. Would you?"

Kate stood up and we watched her join the other two going along the walk.

Before they went through the door, Cronk began to nag at the sheriff. "Now look here, you got me out on a limb, Toland. "I may be on the hook for operating as an M.D. under a diploma mill license, but that's a hell of a way from a murder charge. I demand that you get to the bottom of—"

"You don't demand anything of me, Cronk," Toland said shortly. "One of the things I don't need around here is someone telling me my job. We're making progress. Slow, maybe, but sure. If you didn't kill Engle you can spend all of your time worrying about what you'll tell the medical examiners; we're not going to railroad you on the killing. On the other hand, Cronk, maybe you did have a hand in giving Engle his send-off. In that case, mister, you're in for plenty of trouble. In the meantime all I'll need from you is peace and quiet. I can handle this job, and I will. You got that, Cronk?"

Cronk nodded and Toland turned to me. "So far, Bowman, you've insisted that you weren't even acquainted with Engle; you're clear because you had no reason. That right?"

"Yes."

"You're strictly a friend of Miss Weston? How long have you two been chasing around together?"

This was going to be easy. In those first few miles of the trip up here Kate and I had agreed on our check points. I'd stick to that script and be on safe ground, but along with that I could build us both in solid with Toland if I played it right. I let a grin spread over my face.

"Kate and I met over three months ago." I reflected a moment, then said, "Almost four, now. Jim Spencer, a friend of mine has a steady and they worked out this double date, you see, and—"

"What's that girl friend's name, Bowman? Spencer's girl, I mean."

"Helen," I answered brightly, and tried to hide how glad I was he'd asked. Then I dribbled along, carefully working in all the points we'd set up. It made a fairly plausible situation and Toland seemed satisfied. He let that angle cool off and worked on the Pilchers a while, but the newly liberated fat boy wasn't going to talk much. He was convinced that George Engle's information had gone up the flue and sounded determined to stick by his first statement—simply a friend up for the weekend.

Toland was still getting nowhere with Pilcher when Miss Birch came down the walk with Kate. Her report was short and negative. Mrs. Engle had concealed nothing on her person.

"Uh-huh. Now Miss Weston, I've been going over some items with Mr. Bowman here, and I'd like to check with you. Bowman tells me you two have been running around for over three months and—" The sheriff went on easily, and I had to admit I had thought he was sharper than he appeared at the moment. He didn't change a thing, didn't alter a name or try to trap Kate. He wasn't even watching me to be sure I didn't prompt her a little. He just talked along, working in the facts I'd recited for him and which Kate and I had previously agreed upon.

But halfway through I caught the pitch. He was keeping it straight and honest. When he made the shift she was going to be off the deep end. I closed my eyes and waited, and then I heard Toland's voice grow louder. I looked up to see he'd turned my way, was watching me, but he still spoke to Kate.

"You two seem to agree on everything, but I still think you're holding back. I think George Engle himself invited Bowman up here. And I'll tell you when. According to Mrs. Engle, George was in town one week ago Monday, until late at night. Bowman says that you and he had dinner alone at a place called Karl's, on Wilshire out around Western Avenue. Me, I don't believe you two were alone. I think that you and Bowman met George Engle there for dinner and Bowman is lying when he says he didn't know Engle until yesterday."

"No. We had dinner alone," Kate said. "At Karl's, just as Marty said, and George wasn't—" She stopped then. The look on Toland's face was enough to tell her she'd tripped.

"Now wait a second," I cut in, hoping to blast one past him. "Karl's is a popular place. I eat there often and it just happens—"

Toland held up a hand. "Not on Monday you didn't. I like to have a bite there myself when I'm in L.A. and I know the place pretty well—enough to know you're caught off base. It's closed on Mondays, son. I guess it's about time for someone to make a nice clean breast of things. We could start with you."

"No, let's start with me," Kate said softly. "I—have been guilty of a lot of false answers, I'm afraid. I must have been blessed with an oversupply of concern for other people's business, because Mr. Bowman is a detective and I brought him up here to find out some things for me."

Widdle spoke first. "I'll be damned," he said sarcastically. "A professional nosey. Now I've seen everything."

Eleven

YOU COULD HAVE HEARD the ripples on the pool if there had been any. Toland scratched a leathery ear, then fixed his firm eyes on my face.

"Uh-huh. I got nothing but help around here, it seems, but like I told Cronk, I can get by nicely on my own. You'll limit your hand in this game to answering questions and keeping your fingers out of things. You get that, son?" I nodded and Toland grunted another uh-huh. "We'll start with a look at your license, Bowman."

There wouldn't be any use in tossing Fred's ticket out on the table. I had it; Fred had passed it into my wallet back at Gregory's; something to use for a quick flash if needed, but anything Toland looked at from here on would be strictly under a sharp eye.

"Haven't one," I said simply. "Gregory Agency employed me and the papers haven't gone through yet."

"A little previous, weren't you, taking on work without a card?" I didn't answer, but I was thinking fast. Fred was going to get word to Boreland Gregory when I called last night. By now the fat man must have started the wheels rolling on some kind of ticket for me, if only to protect himself, so it didn't have to be too bad. Vaguely I heard Toland's voice again. "That stuff about you being a lifeguard and all, the part you gave us last night—no wonder it checked out all right. Just went to work for that detective outfit. Well, now, exactly what were you supposed to dig out, Bowman? I guess with the latest developments under our noses we don't have to guess very hard. Miss Weston was under Engle's thumb in a big way, maybe? You were brought up to do something about it and by the looks of things, you certainly filled the bill—once and for all. You got Engle off her back for good."

"Now wait a second, Sheriff. You've got things twisted a bit, and—"

"You haven't said what you were doing up here, son."

"If you'll hold everything for half a second we'll get to that," I said.

Then Kate took over. She put a hand on my arm and her eyes met mine. Then she shook that lovely blonde hair back with a decisive toss of her head.

"Let me do it, Sheriff. I won't lie to you and Marty might, out of chivalry or something. I have never been blackmailed by anyone at any time, and my trips up here were all to see Sandy Engle. We've been friends for years and—" Her warm, soft voice was curiously firm telling Toland the things she had told me about her worries over Sandy and George and the guests at the ranch. Once I'd had difficulty believing her—hadn't believed her, in fact—now she sounded strangely convincing. I could see Toland taking it all in. Now and then her words seemed to filter through a shadow of doubt in his mind, and I could almost see the questions taking shape against the time when he would have to ask them. Right now he wanted to listen.

Outright disbelief was in Bob Widdle's young face but at least part of it made sense to the others gathered around. Most of them could well believe the part about guests being forced to show up at Engle's place. Kate wound it up with a rebuttal to Mrs. Pilcher's story of what had taken place down in front of the café, then stopped for the cross examination we knew would follow.

Toland didn't tee off with as much force as I had expected. He watched us all carefully, then pulled that oversized hat off and gave it his full attention. When he'd reset the crease and put it back on he forced a smile. "It looks like a good day for confessions. Anyone else got something weighing on his chest? I guess we still have most of the questions unanswered, you might say, and someone ought to be able to help us. Cronk?"

"You know why I'm up here. And you know why the rest of them are here too—the same damn reason."

"Not quite all of us," Mrs. Pilcher put in haughtily. "You forget that Dan and I were friends of George. *We* didn't come up here to pay any—"

"We have a minority report on that," Toland said dryly. "Miss Weston's version of the scene in front of the café would seem to indicate that you might have brought a few dollars for an insurance premium when you came."

He drew a nasty look from Mrs. Pilcher but it seemed to worry him little. "Miss Doyle. You've been around the edge of things here for some little time. Exactly what was your connection with Engle?"

Elsa favored the sheriff with a cool brown-eyed look and then let a small smile show through. When she spoke her voice was impersonal and matter-of-fact, and didn't indicate that she cared a damn whether he believed her or not.

"Business, Sheriff. Ironical as it seems, I'm on the other end of the money—George hired me to come here for the weekend."

"He what?" I said and Toland gave me a warning glance.

Then he reworded the question: "How was that, Miss Doyle?"

"It may help solve one of your problems," she said smoothly. "George Engle wasn't exactly what we call a stage-door johnny, but he did know a few people in pictures. My agent, for one. Phil Kegler. George stopped by Kegler's office one day just as I was leaving. We were introduced and a few days later I received a phone call from him, inviting me up for a weekend of relaxation.

I've been here twice since. You see, George always liked to have a house well filled with guests, at least on the weekends, for as Miss Weston has just pointed out, Sandy Engle never leaves here."

"Now wait a minute," Toland said quickly. "Exactly what do you know about Mrs. Engle's not leaving? What besides the things you just heard Miss Weston say five minutes ago?"

"Nothing. Have I said I did?"

"No. But—"

"I'll make it clear once more," Elsa said patiently. "I work for a living. In front of cameras, usually, or in personal appearances, but it all amounts to the same thing —you portray a character. Sandy couldn't—or wouldn't —leave here for some reason, so Engle brought people in. It is obvious, isn't it, that he could have collected his false insurance premiums just as easily in his Los Angeles office? But he didn't, or at least not all of them. Some were asked to come up here for a weekend and bring the cash with them. Why? Surely you can see it as an attempt to keep her from being completely lonely, and a very thoughtful gesture on his part. Quite possibly his list of —of customers included few women. So he hired one now and then. It was, for me, simply a job, a comfortable weekend's work and relaxation. The pay wasn't really in cash, but George always sends a present of some sort after I've been here."

I saw a leer working its way across Pilcher's face. He shifted his toothpick with his tongue and asked, "How big a present, Miss Doyle?" Toland frowned at Pilcher but the redhead didn't need his protection.

"Considerably less than a call girl rate would buy," she said evenly. "And you should see a doctor about those thoughts you're having—a good one, not a Hollywood specialist."

Pilcher turned a deep pink and bit a little harder on

his toothpick as Toland absorbed Elsa's information. When he had, he mentioned that he'd have a word with Mrs. Engle, and that he'd see us later. He waved an arm and started toward the house.

Twenty minutes later I lay on the bed in my room and idly shuffled the six slips of paper with the names I'd written last night. I stood one step ahead of Toland; he had seven because his list would include Marty Bowman, and I had to admit to myself that some of the others were making out better than I at the moment. Still, I knew I hadn't done it.

I shuffled the slips again, then crumpled one and dropped it into the waste basket. Mrs. Pilcher just wasn't clever enough, intense enough, or anything else enough to kill George Engle. I was sure she wouldn't figure very strongly in anything more dire than a P.T.A. installation of officers, and if Danny boy had a finger in this pie it was neither with her knowledge nor her help. It had to be that way.

So there were five. Three beautiful Jills and a pair of overweight Jacks. A full house and one card was willing and able to commit murder if the motive was strong enough. Had already turned the trick, in fact. I smoked in silence and tried to see in and around and under those five people, but there wasn't a single loose end to get a grip on.

The cigarette warmed my fingers and I lit a fresh one from its ember, then ground out the butt. A slow once-over of Elsa's pitch to Toland helped a little. It could have been one hundred per cent opportunism, capitalizing on given facts and building herself into the framework that was already at hand. Toland's observation that she had really added nothing to what Kate had given was well taken—Elsa may simply have carved a spot for herself out of the fact that Sandy was strictly confined to the campus. When she pointed out that George

Engle was providing company for a shut-in wife, she had come up with the most logical deduction of the day.

But why would a man pick this assortment of odd-balls for his weekend guests? Why, besides the cash he could have asked them to drop off at his L.A. office, did Engle invite Cronk? And why Pilcher? Doyle I could understand, and Kate too, assuming she was kidding a little and George was putting the bite on her, but Cronk and Pilcher? Where was this circle of friends the Engles once chased around with down in the city? Where indeed? Who had decided that of them all, only Kate Weston should share the hideaway in the hills overlooking the desert? I kept sliding the facts around and trying to arrange them into some sort of pattern, and when my smoke burned low I ground it against the side of an ashtray, dropped the stub on top of the pile already there, and went toward the door. Before I got my hand on the knob a set of hard knuckles rapped firmly on the wood. When I opened up I was looking at Sheriff Toland.

"Come in," I said, and stepped back. I gestured to a chair, then closed the door and parked on the bed. "You look like a man with something on his mind."

"Not much, Bowman. A very modest amount, to be quite truthful. One buck."

"Oh?"

"Just called my office and the report has come in on that coin Engle had in his hand. A silver dollar, Bowman, with your prints showing through. And don't tell me you and Engle were matching money by that pool at midnight. You can do better than that, I hope. At least, you'd better try."

I tried to grin, then decided there wasn't going to be any way other than telling him the truth. I told him about flipping the buck to decide on a swim before hitting the sack—about going out and all the rest, and then about how I came up here to get into some clothes after Engle was dead and found the dollar missing. We stepped out onto the walk leading around the building on the side next to the hill and I pointed out how someone might have slipped in and picked up the coin. I gave it everything I had, but Toland didn't seem too inclined to buy it, a fact which was more than understandable. When I finished he nodded toward the door and we went back inside.

"Sure, you're wondering why I didn't dash down there and tell you about losing the dollar," I said seriously, "but put yourself in my place for—"

"I'd hate to do that at the moment, son," Toland said grimly.

"You're picking a hell of a time to be funny, Sheriff," I said sharply. "Let's think about last night. There I was —*I'd* pulled Engle out of the pool, *I'd* given him artificial respiration against what we then assumed to be a doctor's advice that he was past help. Moreover, Pilcher and Cronk had lined up against me solidly—had me just about under and I was looking for a way to get my head above water. How could I add to my own troubles by shouting that the thing you found in George Engle's fist was mine? Would you have?"

Toland tried for humor again. "We're not concerned with what I'd have done, lad. I'm about the only one here who has a reasonably good alibi for the time Engle was killed. I was down in Newhall."

"You cheer me, Sheriff," I said without smiling. "If I ever have to organize a minstrel show I'll hire you for an end man."

"Uh-huh. You just let me know what night son, and I'll try to make it. Quite a drive—all the way up to San Quentin, which is where it looks like you'll be. But I'll see what I can do because I wouldn't want to let you down—even then."

"Damn it, Sheriff!" I raged. "You're—" and then the

heat left me, because he was getting through to me now. He'd set out to tilt me a little and he almost made it. I'd been working up to quite a temperature but now I caught the pitch. I gave him a long look, then flicked a thumb toward a chair and flopped out on my bed.

"You've had it, Toland," I said matter-of-factly. "There isn't anything I can add. If you've got any more questions, fire away. If not I'll get a wink or two. The siesta, you'll remember, is an old California custom and I'm strictly a local boy."

Toland glanced at the chair I'd indicated but he didn't sit down. Instead he put a heavy hand on the door, then adjusted his hat. "All right, Bowman. We'll let that do for the present. I'll be running down to Newhall for a while —want to check a few things and get some reports cleared up—but like I mentioned to the others, it wouldn't be a good idea for you to decide to leave here in a hurry. It wouldn't be healthy if Bob Widdle was to hear a car easing down the road—and he'll hear, because they found a room for him over near the garage side of the place. You get the point?"

I said, "Stop trying to put ideas into my head."

"Be either tonight or in the morning when I get back up here, and maybe by then I can pinpoint things and get this over with."

"Take your time." I grinned. "I'm comfortable—and getting paid, remember?" I reached for a magazine on the night stand, then looked up again. "What did the Engle woman say about not getting away from here for the last two years, Sheriff?"

Toland laughed. "I wouldn't want to disturb your siesta, Bowman. See you later today or maybe tomorrow." The door closed after him. I listened to his measured footfalls, then dropped the magazine on the floor and stood up, eased out the back way, and padded over to

Kate's door. I tapped softly, then stepped across the threshold as she swung the door open.

"Hello, Marty." She smiled, but it was definitely not a gay affair. I looked past her and saw Sandy Engle sitting on the white bedspread, her legs drawn up under her, and her white pleated skirt spread over most of her pale legs. Black patent-leather pumps lay on the floor near the bed. I nodded to her and noticed signs of recent tears in her face.

"Could we include one more?" Kate asked, looking at Sandy. "I'm sure Marty wouldn't worry about—about anything." I glanced at Kate, and back at Sandy. She searched my face for several seconds, then lowered· her eyes.

"Go ahead. It's all right, I guess."

"Now wait a second," I said good-naturedly, "I didn't mean to break in on anything. I'll just—" I was backing toward the door but Kate slipped a hand into mine and gave it a quick pressure.

"No. I want to tell you about Sandy because maybe you'll have an idea or two. Toland knows. None of the others, though, because the sheriff was afraid they would all seize it as an excuse to demand that he let them go immediately."

"Seize what as an excuse?" I asked softly.

Kate sat down on a small studio couch along the wall and I parked next to her. "A lot of things have cleared up in the last few minutes," she said quietly. "The reason Sandy hasn't left here in two years is simple—and unfortunate. In fact George built this home for her—two years ago, when a routine medical check-up showed a positive chest X-ray."

I leaned back against the wall and let a slow, low whistle escape. "How bad, Sandy?" I asked. "What's the present situation?"

"Two spots. One large and one quite small. I've had regular checks since and there doesn't seem to be any change, no activity since we came up to the high desert air. I hope you won't think I've been heartless—exposing people to something like this but—"

"Now, wait." I grinned. "We're not going to worry over that. The average person doesn't think about it often, but every time you get on a crowded bus you can count noses and bet that several of those present have at one time had a spot or two. Inactive, sure, but the scar tissue will still show up on an X-ray. Actually, I understand that the chances of passing it aren't too great if reasonable care is taken. All of us have been exposed to active cases at one time or another, of course, and—"

"I know," Sandy said miserably, "but it wasn't a nice thing to think about. When we found—this condition, George and I went down and discussed what to do and how treatment is handled with the doctor. I couldn't face those months, maybe years in a sanitarium, Marty. It almost seemed better to live in town and settle for a shorter time, than go into isolation like that. Then George decided to build here and see if it would help. He sent me to a place for a few weeks and spent a fortune getting immediate construction underway up here. And we didn't tell anyone. George invited people from time to time, but always someone from his business, I thought. I mean I had no idea that his clients were—"

"And then?" I put in, hoping to keep her away from an attack of the weeps over the blackmail business.

"Well, he had these friends come up and we played bridge and sat around the pool, but I didn't get close enough to any of them to—hurt anybody."

"Except George. He wasn't worried?"

"No—he loved me, Marty. A very great deal, I guess, to do what he did. And I let Kate come up. George said that was all right. 'Just the two of us,' he'd say, 'the ones who love you enough not to feel worried—' and that's the way it was. Kate was so healthy and I made certain that I didn't touch her or—"

"Sure," I said.

"You poor dear," Kate said softly. "Of course it didn't matter. You must have felt pretty much left out of things, staying up here alone."

"But I was careful. Please believe me, Kate. I let those friends of George visit us, and you, but—"

"I know," Kate said softly. "You didn't even use the pool except after everyone else had finished."

"Yes. Sometimes at night, just before the water was changed, I'd take a dip. George didn't worry about it; he went in with me, but we never used the pool except at those times. And of course I did very little of that. No violent exercise, you see. I have to conserve all of my energy, the doctor said, and not exert myself."

For one brief moment an idea skittered across the surface of my mind. "Did our friend Cronk do your X-ray work?" I asked quickly. And almost before I finished asking I knew that the facts wouldn't fit—couldn't possibly be consistent.

"No. It was a Hollywood place, Marty. Why?"

"Nothing, I guess. Just an idea that didn't jell." But I kept trying to rework the thing, make a case out of it, because some little facet I couldn't quite put a finger on was beginning to bother me. "You've had X-rays since then, you say? They show no advance?"

"None. The threat is there—always over my head— but I've taken excellent care of myself and George looked after me. I've taken it easy, extremely easy, and the only times I've left here were every three months for a short ride to Newhall. As soon as I was through with the X-ray we came back up here."

"Yeah," I said softly. "You've followed the rest and relaxation routine all right. For sure."

We talked along, and I gave the whole thing a light treatment, tried to keep it on the level of something not the least bit important. By the time I left, Sandy Engle was in a reasonably comfortable frame of mind and at the door Kate flashed me a look of appreciation. "See you later, Marty," she said. "We could take a dip in the pool if you like."

"Sure," I said. "After siesta." Then I went back to my own room but I had no idea of corking off. Instead I wanted to lean back with a cigarette in my hand and blow smoke rings at the ceiling and work over the new information. No, Sandy wasn't being kept up here. She was a victim of something any one of us could stumble into, only George Engle had the dough and enough love for his wife to make things as painless as possible.

But that called for a measure of kindness in Engle, a compassion which was singularly lacking as far as the rest of mankind was concerned. It could be that Engle had focused his love a trifle more than most men do, put it all in one basket and to hell with the rest of the world. I wondered about that too, as I opened the door of my own room and let myself in, then stopped short.

Elsa Doyle was sitting on the arm of an empty chair.

Twelve

VERY CAREFULLY, I closed the door behind me.

"Hello," I said softly. I'd have liked to come up with something sharp, but I couldn't seem to manage it. She'd decked out for the occasion, a set of sheer nylons, spike heels, and a strapless deal in chartreuse that didn't leave you with the least doubts about what was holding it up. She lounged lazily across the arm of the overstuffed, a

cigarette carelessly held in the fingers of her left hand
as she looked up at me. She put the smoke to her lips
and took a long and deliberate drag, then blew the white
cloud to one side.

"Surprised, Marty?"

"Why, no," I said. "I hardly ever step into my room
without finding a half a dozen movie queens parked on
the furniture. It's standard operating procedure." Then I
grinned at her. "If my mouth seemed to hang open there
for a while it must have been my adenoids."

She awarded me a smile. "I wanted to talk to you,
Marty. I'm worried. Maybe being a man you haven't
thought too much about it but George was murdered,
you know, or at least we're reasonably sure he was, and
Toland doesn't seem to be able to find out who's behind it. I'm getting scared." She tried a smile for size and
it didn't fit. "A small chill is starting to creep up my spine."

"Maybe it's that dress," I said. I shook out a cigarette
and found a match. "You don't go along with the obvious
reason for Engle's death, then?"

"You mean—"

"I mean he was putting the bite on someone who bit
back. One of us was paying him off and the tariff got too
steep. You could borrow a line from industry and say
that Engle priced himself right out of business. What
else?" I watched her and tried to figure what kind of a
curve she was pitching. I could see her being shrewd,
or coy, or witty, or even outright sexy if the time was
right, but there was one thing I couldn't see her being
and that was scared. "*You* aren't getting paid for keeping still about anything, are you, Elsa?" I asked pointedly.

"Of course not, Marty." She said it half accusingly and
those serious brown eyes caught my face and held on.

"Then why worry? Relax. Let Toland burn the midnight oil; he's paid for it."

She reached for an ashtray, flicked the gray off her

cigarette, and settled back on the arm of that chair. I took a quick look at my watch and stood up. Kate had mentioned a swim. She could be along any moment now and I didn't want to have her break in on this. She didn't own me, either body or soul, but she was paying for my time and it might complicate things if she thought I was giving the redhead a play. I took a thoughtful drag, then said, "As to who's behind it, Elsa, I guess your opinion will match the next one. If you count noses there are seven possibilities, which means that six of us who are clear must each regard every other member of the team as a possible killer. Only one out of the seven is sure who's guilty and he's not singing it from the rooftop. But I don't agree that Toland isn't getting along with his work. Me, I'm willing to believe he'll point the finger any moment now, but just for the pure hell of it, I'm trying to beat him to the draw. Mentally, that is. It's like sitting in an easy chair in your own living room, a highball in one hand and a smoke in the other, watching a TV quiz show, and trying to outguess some jerk who's standing there in front of nine hundred people. You guess, and when you miss no one is the wiser—you get it right and you feel good all evening." I looked at my watch again, obviously this time, and jerked a thumb toward the pool. I had to get Elsa out of here and the path seemed as good a place as any. "There's a little checking I wanted to do out here before dinner." I smiled. "You got nothing better to do, why not come along, if only for laughs?"

She stood up and dropped the lipstick-stained cigarette stub into the tray. "Sure, Marty. Just for kicks."

We circled the Engle plunge and walked along the narrow strip next to the Cypress trees, then down the flagstones toward the lower end of the grounds. It was like strolling through the park with your best girl on your arm, except that the thoughts occupying my mind were a long way from romance. I had peddled her a bill of goods about Toland, made it sound as if he would reach into the bag and pull out the murderer any second now, but I wasn't quite sold on it myself. I was more than a little worried that the collar he'd get his hand on was the one around my neck.

We walked slowly, the redhead matching her pace to mine, and she asked a casual question about the beaches I'd worked and how many you have to haul out in a season as lifeguard and did many of them survive. I got the feeling she was filling in time, laying a smoke screen and before long she asked what I really knew about Kate Weston. I hedged, then changed the subject, but by the time we came to the bench under the jacaranda she'd worked it back to Kate again.

"About all I can tell you, Elsa, is what I said when the sheriff caught me off base this morning." I grinned. "I thought it was painfully obvious to all hands that I knew damn little about her."

"Come off it, Marty!" She laughed. "It's quite plain that you're more to her than hired help. It shows in her eyes. You can kid Toland, maybe, but any woman would be able to guess."

"You picked the right word, Elsa. A guess, a wild shot, because I'm just a beach bum working from one season to the next and it would take two weeks of my pay to buy a set of tires for that Cad we drove up here in. She's a class lass and I'm just one of the boys from down on the sand, and any other interpretation you hang on us is strictly out of the dream pipe." I tapped the bottom of my pack and held it out to her, then fished out my lighter and snapped the flame alive. "Sit down, Red," I said. "It's my turn. I'd like to ask the questions for a while."

"Of course."

"What's the angle, kid?" I asked with a smile. "What are we trying to achieve at the moment?"

"I don't quite follow you."

"You're way ahead," I said softly. "I'm the boy who's trying to catch up. Why did you stop by my room? Why the questions? Where are we going?"

"You mean you think—"

"Look, Elsa. Let's not kid one another. Your name is in lights and you're on the way up. You need Marty Bowman in your life like you need an extra nose, yet you go out of your way to throw in with him. For a while, and for a reason. It has to be that way."

She gave me a thoughtful look, her deep brown eyes measuring every inch of my face. Then she came up with: "You have, I suppose, seen the rest of the male contingent in this asylum?"

"Pilcher and Cronk?" I grinned. "There's a lot of man divided up between those two."

"Enough suet for three ordinary men, Marty. You really shouldn't be proud to stand out in that kind of company, you know. I—like you. Put me down as a lover of brown-skinned blonds with muscle. There's your reason and as to the time, we're both too young to worry much about tomorrow. Right?"

"The tide must have changed on me," I said evenly. "I thought you were plenty worried a few minutes ago. You said so."

"Marty, you're being mean!" She pouted. "Couldn't we just talk for a while without jumping at each other's throats?"

"Maybe we can." I smiled. "You know, living as close to the movie industry as I do in L.A. I still don't know a hell of a lot about it. Like how some of you kids break in and all. You, for instance—where did you get a break and how long had you been plugging at it before the door opened?"

She started to talk about her movie career then, and it gave me time to think about a few other things. But somewhere along the line I climbed back into the boat and began to pay strict attention to Elsa, because the words were striking a familiar chord. Like a record you've heard before, and it shouldn't have been—not when you talk about your own life. One day you see things one way and the next day differently—you're likely to accent certain things or alter the order, or omit incidents you stressed earlier. But some bit of business that you've learned by rote comes out the same every time, and from Elsa Doyle I was getting a replay of the recitation she'd given Toland. It reminded me of the brush salesman they used to tell about. He memorized his entire sales talk from start to finish. If someone interrupted his spiel and threw him off the track he had to go back out and rap on the door again and start from his opening sentence. Not that the red-headed bundle of curves sitting under the jacaranda tree was dull. You couldn't say that by any stretch of your imagination, but she was being careful to hew to the line, keeping her story straight.

When she finished I held out a hand. She took it, and I helped her up. We went slowly toward the pool again, our steps uneven as we followed the brown flagstones. Elsa managed to keep her fingers linked through mine and as we neared the opening in the row of cypress she held back, then faced me as I turned toward her.

"We've gotten to know each other ever so much better, Marty." She smiled. "But you haven't told me what you've uncovered so far. You were coming out here to find out something. What were you looking for?"

"Information," I said vaguely.

"About?"

"You," I said lightly, then took the edge off with a big round grin. "Just checking up."

She drew back and gave me a mild look. "That sounded like something said a little bit in jest and a whole lot in earnest, Marty," she said slowly. "You mean—"

She stopped then as footsteps sounded along the walk. Heavy steps. The tubby threesome came through the row of trees and walked past us. I gave a curt nod and it was not returned. In fact the only recognition I received was a slight uptilting of Mrs. Pilcher's nose as she passed, but the babe next to me made out a great deal better. Pilcher was sneaking sidelong glances at her underpinning as he closed on us and so was Cronk, and when they were fifty feet down the flagstone walk Dan Pilcher turned for a quick stern-view. I watched them go, my mind ticking off possible ways to wriggle off the hook with Elsa.

"Just kidding, of course." I let my eyes grow serious. "It's like Toland said. Someone slipped a towel around Engle's neck and sort of hampered his breathing for a while. The sheriff says it would have to have been a reasonably strong person and he's eliminated the girls. I'll go along with that—there isn't any reason to doubt it. Do you think so, Elsa?"

"I don't know." She grew thoughtful for a few seconds, then nodded in the direction Pilcher, his wife, and Cronk had disappeared. "They seem to be friends again, Marty. I wonder."

"In union there is strength, they say. Maybe they're sharpening the knife for Bowman." I took her arm then and piloted her through the cypress and around the edge of the pool. We walked slowly toward the house and I dropped Elsa in the main hallway, went on to my own room, slipped into a pair of trunks, and picked up a towel. When I got back to the pool, Kate Weston was just

draping her white terrycloth beach robe over the back
of a deck chair.

"Busy day, little man?" she asked dryly.

"Business," I said shortly. "Strictly business."

"Nice, if you can get it—and it looks like you could."

"Let's swim." I said, and cut into the blue warmth of
Engle's fancy pool. I slid through the water and enjoyed
the feel of it against my hands as I swam, felt its pressure
along my body and legs. Catching the tile drain-trough
on the far side, I turned and pushed off and stroked back
to the edge where Kate stood, then looked up at her.
She was tucking that beautiful blonde hair under the rim
of a white rubber bathing cap and I hadn't seen this swim
suit before. Two-piece, all white lastex—considerably
more coverage than those bikini jobs but still brief
enough to be plenty interesting. The upper part was one
of those no-strap bras that depend a little on the cut of
the cloth and a lot on the curve of the chassis to keep
them in place. For diving there was an auxiliary neck
band that tied behind.

It crossed my mind that it must have set her back
about twenty clams, even wholesale, which would be the
way she'd get it—then remembered that we people with
half of all the money in the world don't put things in
terms of what they cost. When she snapped the chin band
in place she arched over my head and slipped through
the surface with hardly a sound and very little splash. A
true water fan, this blonde. I caught her as she turned
to make the pool the long way and together we swam
through the tepid water. We stopped momentarily under
the diving board, then hit a mutual cadence as we
stroked toward the shallow end, and in the forward
glance you take just after you roll your head up to in-
hale, I saw that Toland's boy, Bob Widdle, had come
down to keep an eye on things.

I grinned to myself. He hadn't come to pick up any

points on swimming. You didn't have to be a student of
form to appreciate the tan loveliness poured into that
two-piece swim suit Kate was wearing and Widdle was
human—and maybe a year or two younger than Marty
Bowman. Put him at the end of the twenties, a big boy
with a likeable rural slant on life, and an open face.

Kate and I made half a dozen more lengths of the
pool, thinking our own thoughts, yet matching stroke for
stroke in a lazy, measured pace that was almost restful.
I fell to drawing comparisons between my blonde and the
carefully groomed redhead with a film career in the making. The one an upper-crust chick with money in the
family—a fancy women's apparel shop in Hollywood
and a Caddy to sport around in when she wasn't sitting
at a desk in daddy's shop and giving orders to the help.
The other, the starlet, obviously self-made and bucking
her way up in the toughest competition the world can
toss at a girl. Discounting part of her pitch as the usual
malarky the publicity department at the studio would
grind out, there were still enough facts to tell you that
Elsa Doyle was willing to battle her own way in the
world. And able—looking back at our brief session together I got the feeling that she was cultivating Bowman
for a reason. A fairly specific reason, it looked like, because she wouldn't have to work hard to impress her
physical charms on a male. Nature had taken care of
that. Maybe she thought that by hanging around she
might stumble onto some little angle that could be ex-
ploited for publicity—she might even palm off a solution
to Engle's death as her own and it would put her on page
one for a week. It seemed logical, and then my grin
broadened because I thought of something else. I had
our Elsa pegged for the kind that was out to parlay sex
into a career one way or another, and I hadn't the least
doubt that, if a desirable role in some film were at stake,

our Elsa would indulge what Hollywood has come to know as the casting couch.

Well, hell. Marty Bowman could be talked into giving credit where credit wasn't due. Me, I don't need publicity.

Thirteen

KATE AND I had the pool to ourselves, and for the better part of an hour we enjoyed it. We took a few from the springboard and when we tired of that, pulled a couple of green pads next to each other and let the afternoon sun spirit away the water in our bathing suits. Kate slipped off her rubber cap and shook that long golden hair over her shoulders, folded an elbow and rested her cheek on the back of her hand, then smiled across at me.

"I think you've got a secret admirer," I said, my voice low. "The sheriff's understudy hasn't turned a page of that magazine in his lap for ten minutes."

Kate wrinkled her nose, rolled over for a look at Widdle who sat in a deck chair just past the far end of the plunge. She turned back to me.

"Just one?" She let a smile play across the corner of her tan face, her blue eyes wandering off to the side a little.

"That's all. One. The other guy isn't making any secret of it," I said.

She touched the tip of her finger to her chin and gave me a quick look. "Nice recovery."

"It's no recovery. I haven't changed my mind since yesterday. On the way up here—when I said you're blonde and beautiful and all the rest. When I make my first million I'll look up Weston's Women's Apparel and drop in to see you."

"Marty, I—" She stopped there, then pressed her lips tightly together and turned away.

"What's on your mind, Kate?"

"Nothing, I guess. You—well it isn't going to matter, I suppose. How about the situation here? We'd better talk about that, instead of getting all tangled up in personalities."

"Yeah," I said. I got up and walked around the pool to where I'd tossed my smokes, brought the pack and my lighter back and flopped down again. When we were half-way through our cigarettes I'd made a strong decision. It was just about twenty-four hours since I'd parked her Cad on the strip beside Engle's place and something less since I had pulled our host's lifeless body out of the water. A hell of a lot had been brought to light about those gathered in that time, but if Toland had made any real progress he was keeping it under his hat. It didn't seem like a bad policy. For several hours now a nagging little thought had tugged at my mind but there wasn't any reason to spill it to Kate. If I was right it would look like a real sharp operation later and if I was off base—wound up doing a belly-flop—I'd feel less silly if I hadn't sounded off. Much better to work along quietly for a while. I started by putting the pump on Kate.

"Would you remember, just offhand, any of the other guests you've met up here from time to time?" I asked.

She gave me a questioning glance, then shook her head. "No, I don't think so. Why?"

"Try hard. No names, nothing you could put a finger on and recall what they looked like or talked like or what they did?"

She thought it over for a while. "I guess I could get a name here or there, but it would be pretty hard to connect the names to the people if someone paraded the entire list in front of me, Marty. I just haven't noticed, I suppose. Maybe if you could tell me exactly what it was you wanted to know, I'd be able—"

"Thanks. You've answered already. For once something around this wacky ward is making sense. Maybe good sense, and if it turns into anything I'll cut you in. Fair enough?"

"Fair enough," she echoed, and I cradled my head on my crossed arms and started to think. One loose end. one little thread sticking out of the tangle, and maybe. . . .

It took a while to lay the foundation but by the time dinner was over I had something solid in the making. I got up when Kate left the table and followed her into the hall, and when she turned to lift a questioning eyebrow I nodded toward her room, then stepped in after her and closed the door.

"Feel like an evening swim?" I asked.

"Sure, Marty. Say when."

"Now. But not with me. I was thinking maybe you'd go it solo for a while."

She leaned against the top of a dressing table and gave me the full treatment with those soft blue eyes. "You were going to cut me in," she invited.

"When I get something," I said. "Remember? So far I'm as close as I am to flying to the moon. Now be a good kid and climb into that fetching white bathing suit, what there is of it, and go take a few dives. It would help if you can manage to look at Widdle now and then."

She smiled, then let it grow into a grin. "You wouldn't by any chance be thinking—"

"How about those dives?" I cut in. "Say about twenty minutes from now?"

"Marty." She came toward me, her eyes asking the question before her lips framed the words. "Marty, it isn't Elsa, is it? You're not going to see her, or get out of here with her, or—"

I put a stop to the questions in the only sensible way a man could. My arms tightened around Kate's slim waist and I pressed her to me, kissed her full and hard on those soft upturned lips and felt their warm answer. A number of seconds passed, every one of them wonderful, and when we parted I stroked her hair and smiled down at her.

"I missed a lot of words yesterday," I said. "Blonde and beautiful weren't even a good start. We'll have to go into the rest of it some night. Maybe tonight—a little later?"

"A little later, Marty," she said. I kissed her again, reminded her to hurry into that bathing suit, and let myself out.

A little later I rapped on Sandy's door. Five minutes more and I was back out on the terrace. Widdle had his magazine again, but now he managed to turn a page every once in a while. I stood beside him and struck a flame, lit my smoke and flipped away the match.

"What do you hear from Toland? He coming back tonight?" I asked.

"Haven't any idea, Bowman. Why?"

"Well, I was thinking of hitting the sack," I said. I wrinkled my forehead and pressed the palm of my hand to my face. "Too much sun, maybe. Just thought I'd tell you, in case anyone wants me. Okay?"

He gave me a quick hard look, then nodded and went back to his reading. I wandered toward the house, went into the main hall, and then stopped in the living room. I thumbed through a day-old paper until the hands on my watch said seven, stood up, and eased over to the large picture window overlooking the terrace and pool. Kate Weston was poised on the diving board and Widdle's magazine had reached a new low on his lap. I grinned to myself and slipped through the house toward the garage, then out to the big Cad. When Sandy Engle came quietly up to the car I opened the door for her, then closed it noiselessly and slid in behind the wheel. Releasing the hand brake, I let the heavy wagon roll back and when it had gone a few feet I cramped her hard left, kept an eye on the edge of the concrete, then pressed lightly on the brake. She stopped and then, as I released the brake pressure and whipped the wheel to the right, the Cad started down the hill. We let gravity do the honors for half a mile, then wound up the engine and slipped the hydromatic into drive. At the canyon highway we pulled onto the concrete and swung north, the heavy hack rolling smoothly over the road. The summit, then the winding pavement toward Palmdale, and the wan brunette beside me flashed a dubious look my way.

"This is crazy," she said at last. "It's only been three months since my last check-up. There could hardly be much change in that time. Not enough to show. And in the second place it's Saturday night—after seven and you certainly won't find a lab open at this hour."

"You came, though," I observed dryly.

"Yes. Hope against hope, Marty—if there's even a chance that you might be right, but—"

"No buts. Leave it to Bowman, Sandy."

"But if they're not open?"

"We'll open 'em."

"You don't lack confidence, do you, Marty?"

I didn't say any more about it and we talked about other things—the years she and Kate had chased around together, her marriage, some of the people she knew back in the city. It was nearing eight when we slid to a stop beside a drugstore in Lancaster. I checked the phone book for an address, then asked the waitress how to get there. We found the X-ray lab locked.

" 'We'll open 'em,' " she taunted. I got out and went up

to the door, my eye searching for the emergency address sign most any shop has pasted down in one corner. There were two names—the doctor who must have owned the place and a Mr. Kelson with a phone number and an address. He'd be the technician, our target for tonight. I scribbled his house number and street on a card, then drove to a gas station, took on ten gallons and asked directions.

It wasn't far. A few minutes later I was rapping on the door of a modest concrete block bungalow near the edge of town. My third try brought a freckle-faced lad of about ten around the side of the house.

"Pa's out in back. We're gonna barbecue," he said happily.

I followed him along the new cement walk, through a white wooden gate, and over to the far corner of the lot. A red brick patio bearing unmistakable signs of an amateur's hand stood against a not yet completed block fence and a thin gent in faded Army fatigues bent over the flames of a wood fire. When he turned to give me a 'howdy' I guessed him to be in the early thirties, the gaunt type who, due to premature baldness, probably looked a little older than he really was. On the flat brick counter near him were red hamburger patties, a cellophane package of buns, catsup, and a bottle of hickory sauce.

"Mr. Kelson?"

"That's right." He set down a bag of charcoal and dusted his hands on the legs of those faded green fatigues.

"Marty Bowman," I said. Then: "Your name was on the card down at the lab. How about a little overtime tonight?"

"Emergency? And from which doctor, Mr. Bowman?"

"No emergency. Routine chest X-ray. But I need it now."

"Well, I'd sure like to help you, but unless it's something that can't wait—broken bones or like that, brought
in by a physician—we don't open up. You drop by in the
morning at nine and I'll get you first thing."

"Not me. A friend of mine, and we can't wait."

"What's so urgent about a chest X-ray? And you'll
need an M.D. to read it anyway, you know. We can't
just—"

He stopped talking when I brought out my wallet and
slid a twenty into my hand. Then I folded the bill length-
wise like a crap shooter and looked at Kelson.

"Time is money, Mr. Kelson," I said, "and we're in a
hurry. I just want the plates—we'll worry about getting
the thing read later."

Kelson's eye was following the green bill and I knew
he was beginning to see the light. He raised an eyebrow,
then glanced toward his unfinished fence and back to the
cash again. It wasn't hard to guess he was seeing twenty
more dollars worth of blocks in that wall. I let the bill
waft to the ground and was a little slow in bending for it.
He got there first. When he straightened up with the cash
in his hand, he turned to the freckle-faced lad beside
him.

"Tell your mother to hold those french fries back for
about forty minutes. You can drop some of this charcoal
on the fire now and it'll be down to coals when I get back.
And don't get burned, hear?" He winked at me
and walked toward a pre-war Chevvy parked in his driveway.

He looked a lot different in a white jacket. Sandy came
out of the dressing room, a plain short hospital gown cov-
ering the part above her skirt as she stepped in front of
the shining black glass plate.

I held out a tiny safety pin. "Stick it in the cloth. Low,
but not too far down."

She looked curiously at the pin, then fastened it in the gown. Kelson gave her that breathe-and-hold-it routine twice, then went to process the plates. By the time he came out with them, Sandy was dressed. He handed me the oversized brown envelope, took the ten dollar bill I held out, and began to rummage for change.

"Eight dollars, Mr. Bowman. I'll get—"

"Skip it. Tomorrow you can barbecue steak. On Gregory."

"Thanks. Thanks, but on who, did you say?"

"You don't know him, but he's still stuck for it. Good night."

"Well, thanks." Kelson said, and the door closed after us.

We got into the car and rolled back to the drugstore, and this time I checked for doctors. Phoning several, I was able to get appointments with two who were home and would see us. The first turned out to be a round little character with a penchant for using more words than were necessary and reasonable. Sandy and I sat down in the office he maintained in the front part of his house and the doctor beamed at us.

"Ah, yes. Always nice to see two young people so well matched. A blond boy and brunette girl, a nice combination indeed. And now what was this about an X-ray? You have it with you, I see."

"We thought that might help." I smiled.

He favored me with a questioning glance, then chuckled. I slid the envelope across his desk.

"We'd like you to go over these, if you would. We'll wait."

"Certainly, certainly. Hmmm. Chest X-rays, eh. Yes indeed."

"That's right, Doc, for one dollar. Like to try for two?"

He couldn't be ruffled. "A quiz program fan, eh?

Say, I was listening to a pretty good one the other night.
Fella was asked—"

The doc yacked on while he was getting his light set
up, but I'll have to admit that when he put the plate up
against the illuminated ground glass, all nonsense ceased.
He even forgot what the sixty-four dollar question was.
Taking the first plate off, he studied the second, then
called us over.

"You aren't joking, Mr. Bowman? I mean that pin I
see is really in the blouse—or was, wasn't it?"

"Certainly. Don't worry about the pin. The lady put
the pin there to be sure there wasn't any switching of film.
All we want to know is the condition of the chest. The
spots. Are they active or bottled up or what?"

The doctor didn't even glance back at the plates.
He sat his round bottom on the nearest chair and gave
us a big grin. "What are we playing, Mr. Bowman? Nobody can say I won't go along with a gag, but—"

"There isn't any gag. What about the X-ray?" I said it
in a hard flat voice and when he turned his smile my way
I didn't bounce back with one. His face straightened and
he went back to the plate still on his glass, then motioned us over with his finger.

"This is a pin. You said it was on the dressing gown
so we don't have to worry about that, eh? Now as far as
the rest of this X-ray goes, there isn't a sign of any chest
condition; no scar tissue, even. There is not now, nor
has there ever been any tubercular infection in these
lungs."

"Thank you, Doctor. We'll take the films with us, if you
don't mind." I slid them back into the envelope and
dropped one of Boreland Gregory's twenties on the desk.
The doc scribbled a receipt and piled a few bills on
top of it, and Sandy and I left without half hearing
the patter the doc dished out as we went down the walk.

When we got back into Kate's big Cad I looked across at Sandy Engle.

Her eyes were faraway, her head tipped back against the gray leather, and in the half-light I saw the mixed emotions bubbling up from the depths.

"How can I tell you what I feel?" she asked softly. "I saw those other plates, Marty. I sat in a doctor's office and watched while he traced those shadows. But now—"

"You put that pin in the gown tonight," I said, easing the car out into the street. "With your own hands, Sandy. I didn't arrange it in the cloth; just gave the thing to you, and you saw it on the plate just the way you had it when he took the picture. There was no possible way I could have switched X-rays. Which means?"

"I know. The other time was the phoney, Marty. But how? I mean—"

"Some of it I can tell you, Sandy. Some we can guess, but the rest you'll have to throw in for me. As to the how, there's one way it could have been done, and quite easily. Engle couldn't get Cronk to turn this job. That would have put the doc in position to demand something from George. Hell, if Cronk had known that George was keeping you there—but he didn't. It was a reputable Hollywood physician who read the plate for you, Sandy, but he didn't take it. A local lab did that, and George brought it to the office. Now it's a fair guess that he switched to one he'd gotten from Cronk, but without telling Cronk his reason for wanting it. Simple?"

"Yes—Marty, it must have been like that. But what about the check films every three months? I've had—"

"Just down to Newhall and right back. You got the reports later, didn't you? You said so."

Sandy nodded her dark head slowly. "Yes. And from George."

"Sure. From George."

"George. The one who loved me best," she said in

a strained, mocking voice. "George, who was never afraid to swim with me, never afraid of getting—"

"Now take it easy, Sandy."

"Take it easy? Two years, Marty. Do you put someone in jail for two years, frighten her and then say it was all a mistake and to take it easy?"

I said sternly, "You're getting worked up unnecessarily. That little collection of flagstone and concrete you've got in the hills might be made of the same materials as a jail but it's arranged a hell of a lot differently. You'd best calm down a little, Sandy. I'll phone that second doctor. There's no use keeping the other appointment—if you're satisfied as to what's on the plates."

"Phone him, Marty. Phone him from a bar, because that's where you're taking me. Fast. Tonight's the night little Sandy climbs down off the wagon."

"Easy now," I said, smiling. "You could overdo it without too much trouble, you know. You—"

"I hope to shout in your ear I'll overdo it. And tonight. Two years on lemonade. 'You must conserve your energy, Sandy, dear,' and, 'You'll be better off not to drink anything with alcohol, baby,' and, 'You have to be careful, my love,' and—come on, Marty. Let's find that phone."

We cruised slowly along a side street and I tried to grasp the change in Sandy Engle. Before it had been hard to picture her as a running mate for Kate Weston; now it was easy. The shy, retiring, and almost torpid Sandy Engle I had known for just over one day had been that way for a brief two years, pressed into the mold by George Engle, urged to avoid any kind of close contact with others. No wonder Kate Weston had been puzzled. 'Sandy likes to get around,' Kate had said, and, 'Sandy's eyes haven't gotten the word, Marty. She wants to get away.' I could understand that now, could see that two years of pressure had built up in the pale and thin bru-

nette beside me. And it might not be a good idea to let
her break the bonds tonight, but from where I stood
there wasn't going to be a hell of a lot of choice. Engle
had sold her a bill of goods, put her in a hothouse and
kept her there until lack of exercise and interest had cut
away her vitality by sheer inactivity. Now she was out to
recapture two years of living in a single night. I didn't
like the sound of it but I couldn't dredge up more than
one logical line of reasoning to talk her out of it.

"Look, Sandy," I said earnestly. "I can see how you
feel all right, and no one can possibly say you don't rate
a night on the town. A lot of them, maybe, to make up
for the time you've been in exile, but think how this is
going to look."

"Let's talk about how it's going to taste, Marty, and the
sooner the better."

I shook my head, hesitated, then smiled in spite of myself. Sandy could have been a hell of a lot of fun before
George Engle put her under wraps. She might still be
more fun than three drunken monkeys, I guessed, but it
would have to be some other night.

"Put it this way. You've been on the wagon for two
years, Sandy, and a few more days won't hurt. Now
George is dead and he was your husband. No matter
how sore you are tonight or how much you feel you've
been cheated and double-crossed, it still wouldn't look
just—"

"Marty, boy, if what I feel for George tonight were put
into print it would be banned in a lot of places besides
Boston. He—oh, hell, stop being noble. On to the tavern
and a new life."

"But we want to be fair, Sandy. You—"

"To George?" she gave me a scornful look.

"Well, no, but to yourself."

She reached over and patted my shoulder. "In the last
two years, Marty, I've downed enough lemonade to keep

an average-sized orchard in business. Now I ask you, was that quite fair to the farmers who raise rye?" The hand on my shoulder slipped up to my cheek. "You were a hundred per cent right, Marty, lad. We want to be fair. Now can I have that drink?"

"Well, maybe," I hedged, and turned up toward the main street. "We'll try one for size."

"Thanks, Marty." Then her face lost its smile again and she stared into the bright cones of our headlights. "There's a lot of things you don't know about George Engle. Or maybe you do. You seem to have come right along in the time you've been on the grounds. I'd like to know how you figured some of it out, and as you said, I might be able to straighten out a few spots for you. I'd sure like to try."

"You've got yourself a deal, Sandy." I rolled along the main drag for two blocks, then parked the big Cad in front of a cocktail bar and went around to open the door for her. She had that look of eager anticipation in her eye and once again I began to wonder just how good an idea this was and how you shut a determined woman off with a single drink.

Fourteen

It WAS about what you usually find in a bar—dark red leatherette booths with a plastic-topped table big enough to hold four glasses, an ashtray, and the small tray for your change. I managed to stake a claim on one not too far from a neon that gave enough light to enable me to keep an eye on Sandy, something I certainly intended to do. The barhop was cute in a late thirtyish sort of way and walked with an interesting bounce in the right places.

She slid a tiny paper napkin in front of each of us, then placed a pair of coasters on the table and looked up expectantly.

"A whiskey highball, please," Sandy said. She was back in the groove all right; you'd never have pegged this for her first outing in a couple of years. I ordered a daiquiri and the waitress nodded, then went toward the three feet of bar roped off for exclusive use of the help. Sandy Engle put her purse on the seat beside her and leaned toward me.

"How did you know, Marty? You said we'd see if I hadn't maybe been okay for a while, but you didn't really mean that. You weren't surprised when the man said I never even had so much as scar tissue showing."

I gave her a quick wink. "It's a gift. Some have it and some haven't." Dropping one of Gregory's twenties on the change tray I stood up, flipped a thumb toward the phone booth and said, "Be right back."

The doc's line was busy. Standing in the booth, I glanced idly around the bar, my eye stopping on a washed-out blonde near the far side. She'd had just enough to loosen her tongue and so had her escort, a situation mildly humorous to the semicircle of grinning patrons lining the bar, but it wasn't humorous to Bowman. It gave him an idea. I got my call through to the M.D., apologized and said we wouldn't be able to make it after all, heard him thank me for letting him know, and then hung up. Toward the rear were two doors, each with a picture of a dog. One was a black-and-white pointer, the other an Irish setter. I lingered by the phone booth until I caught the bartender's eye, signaled him and went in with the pointers.

"Something wrong, Mac?" he asked as he came in.

"Yeah. With my tummy. Got an ulcer and she's kicking up a fuss but I hate to be a spoil-sport. You know how it is."

"Sure, Mac." He was grinning now.

"I'm ordering daiquiris. I think the one already on the table will be about all I can handle. Let's make the rest of them a weak limeade, shall we?" I fished out a five that had come back in change from one of Boreland Gregory's bigger bills and crossed the barkeep's palm with green.

"Limeades, it'll be, mate. A weak splice for the main-brace."

He folded the five and tucked it into a slit in his white jacket, gave me a half salute, and went out. Damn, I thought, these dry land sailors! He probably had all of sixteen months in the service and fifteen of them on some shore base, but from that day forward the walls were bulkheads, the floors were decks and he never spat to windward.

When I got back to the table Sandy had her white fingers around her drink and my daiquiri had worked up a nice dew on the glass.

"Health," I said, sliding in and lifting my drink.

"And the bright lad who showed me I still have it," Sandy added. We sipped cool liquid, then looked across at each other.

"You were going to tell me how you knew, Marty. And let's be honest with each other; it was definitely more than a hunch."

"Call it an informed guess. An odd here and an end there—they made a pattern."

"Then let's talk about odds and ends."

I touched a finger to my glass and ran it all the way around the rim. "This could get pretty intimate, Sandy. Sex figures in the picture here and there, and the whole thing is a wee bit—delicate. Too delicate to discuss on a single daiquiri."

"If you're suggesting a vote on a second round, count me among those in favor," she said smiling. We looked

at each other through the bottoms. I stalled while we
downed another, this time without the rum, and on the
third I let her pin me down to facts.

"First we take George Engle. Smooth as a beach peb-
ble but under it all very egotistical, as suggested by the
diving tower that wouldn't be put up until he was an expert. Nobody was going to show George up at anything
if he could help it. He had to be the top man. Which
brings us to the guests he invited up to the estate. The
red-headed babe has been with you several times but
none of the males here impressed her very much. And
the same with Kate Weston. She couldn't recall a single
one very clearly. Which points to the fact that none of the
guests were what we might call eligible men. No, the fat
and bespectacled Cronk and his running mate Pilcher
were a fair average sample of the male contingent around
here. You get the idea that any handsome gents under
forty that Engle might have had on the string were making their payments in his L.A. office, not up here where
Mrs. Engle would see them. George was mighty sure
that anyone he invited would add to the attractiveness
of G.E. by direct comparison. Catch?"

Sandy nodded, smiled. "Sharp."

"Actually, no. It took me a while to catch on. Take
this noble business of his of building your desert hideaway.
The milk of human kindness has usually curdled in a
man, I'd guess, before he can bring himself to blackmail
someone, yet wholesale blackmail is certainly more
than suggested. It made me wonder about his being the
kind who would give his all for a wife—even one with
lovely black hair—and many other attractions."

"Thank you kindly, sir. That last part is appreciated.
But you needed three drinks to tell me this?"

"No. They were for the next part. Like the reason he
drummed up to hold you here where attractive men

would be practically non-existent. You were supposed to take it real easy, he said. No violent exercise. No hikes in the hills or such. Tell me, Sandy. Were there any other —exercises—in which our boy George—well, suggested that you'd better cut down a little. I've got the odd notion that, at great personal sacrifice, he may have excused you from some of your wifely duties," I finished with a grin.

Sandy took a sip of her drink and leaned toward me again. For several seconds her eyes went back and forth across my face and then she nodded. "When Marty Bowman looks into the crystal ball he really gets the picture," she breathed softly. "I—can't imagine how you—I mean —" She let it trail off and I took over.

"I'm young and healthy—" I smiled—"and if I wanted to hibernate with a chick I'd scoot off to a tropical isle or find a mountain retreat or maybe even a layout like yours up there, but there's one thing I wouldn't do and that's dream up a dodge which would keep the better half from leading an active life.

"Not that this angle on George came out of thin air," I went on. "It didn't. The night he was—he died—I had been reading while I had a snack. There was a page missing from a physical culture magazine and I found that the other side had one of those rejuvenation ads. Or at least every other issue had that advertisement. The whole page had been neatly cut out and I thought then that someone visiting you people had felt the need of a little extraneous inspiration. Today, though, when Kate and I were sunning ourselves by the pool, I was watching Bob Widdle and he had one of those muscle magazines in his lap and all at once I began to think about that ad. Looked at in the light of George's death and his other odd behavior, I began to be more than a little sure of where that coupon went. George was a lot older than

you, but not that much older, so it wasn't too obvious,
but it could fit. Maybe it wasn't the years but the way
he lived 'em. At any rate it got around to looking like
he'd had a little difficulty and found a smooth way out
of it—put you on the shelf with little or no embarrass-
ment to himself. Real cool—he even appeared noble in
the doing."

Sandy let her eyes fasten on me again. "George.
George Engle—that clever, clever rascal." She said it
carefully, each word pronounced slowly. Too slowly,
and it was the sign I had been looking for. I pushed my
empty toward the center of the table, scooped the re-
maining bills and coins out of the silver tray, dropped a
single for the tip and pointed to Sandy's glass.

"We've had it, kid. That was the one for the road."
I started to slide out of the booth but she leaned across
and put a hand on my arm."

"Now, listen, Marty. Little Sandy has only had three
of these—in two years."

I said, "That's the part we're worrying about, baby.
The water wagon gets higher every day and you've been
riding it a long time. When you fall from that far up you
hit pretty hard. Now be a smart girl and let's get some
air. If we're dying of thirst when we pass through Palmdale we can stop for a booster shot. Deal?" I patted the
white fingers on my arm, then eased her hand off and
stood up.

Sandy picked up her bag, scooted to the open end of
the booth, and then tipped up her glass and sucked the
last few drops out with a gurgling sound. Her mouth
opened, closed again, and she licked her lips. "Oooo,
Marty!"

Grinning, I gave her my arm and on the way out
to the car she leaned a little heavily a time or two. I
swung the door for her, then hurried around to my own

side, hopped in, and wound up the engine. I'd had an idea. Toland seemed to have figured Sandy might be holding out on him about those envelopes with the black-mail evidence. I thought so too, and figured that a few drops of oil applied to the lovely brunette's tongue would loosen it sufficiently to get us on a buddy-buddy footing and she'd cut me in. But I had to pour the lubrication with care, because nothing would be more useless than a boozed-up babe who could pass out on my hands. I was going to watch this pigeon with a sharp eye. Even three might have been too many after so long a drought.

"Oooo, Marty!" she said again. "I'm getting all warm inside." She squealed like a teen-ager standing in the cold surf, then wiggled across the seat and snuggled up against me.

We passed the city limit of Lancaster and I put a bit more weight on the throttle. The Cad responded like no car of my own ever has and we sped toward Palmdale. "A little earlier," I reminded the girl, "we formed sort of a partnership. Something about discussing the odds and ends and filling in for each other on the blank spaces. Remember? So just to paint a better background into the picture, how about a look at this thing from the wife's angle? You could start with the first time George mentioned that you should have an examination."

She said, "Not an examination, Marty. Looking back and considering what we've found out tonight, I can see that it fits together loosely in places. But at the time I didn't—well, take the very beginning. I was tired one night, we'd been on the go all day, but George didn't think I was up to par. He suggested that we both have a chest X-ray just for the comfort we'd get out of knowing that things were all right. He made appointments for us at a regular laboratory and we went down. Then he picked up the films later and we went to a local M.D. for a consultation. As you say, he must have switched plates, though, and—" Sandy went along for a while, adding little that I didn't already know.

"Now about the year you two lived in wedded bliss, Sandy, that first year. How were you getting along? No troubles I guess—like you making eyes at a neighbor or anything?"

She gave me a shrewd side glance and a smile. "Look, old pardner-pardner. You aren't working on a one man Kinsey report are you?" I laughed and she did too. "There might have been a friend or two in our set that I liked a little but I didn't play around any. It might have been in the offing, though, if we hadn't shifted to a hermit's life."

"And George had it figured, I'll bet. He wasn't a damn bit slow in the head, George Engle."

"No, but he wasn't the loving husband either, not all the time. You came close when you mentioned his having to be the center of attraction on every occasion. We had our tiffs. Plenty of them, but when I had my trouble —or he made me think I did—he was so darn nice about it. Building that place in the hills and having people up every week end or so and going into the pool with me. Oh, I was sold on him then all right. God! Two years of my life down the well."

We cruised along and Palmdale loomed ahead. I was vaguely aware that a small game of footsie was developing down around the accelerator. A tiny high-heeled shoe was resting next to my right foot and every now and then an ankle in sheer nylon pressed against the cuff of my flannels. I blew a soft breath and wondered if she could be talked into discussing those white envelopes, then decided that now wasn't the hour. Her glow had been short-lived and needed a recharge; I wanted to get her back on the "Ooooo, Marty!" basis.

"Last chance, Sandy. You seem to handle it with ease

and if you'd like that parting shot—" She gave my arm a warm tight squeeze. We found a likely-looking oasis and when we were comfortably installed in a booth I said "Just one. Then we're on our way. Agreed?"

"Agreed, Marty." And then to the waitress: "I'll try a whiskey cobbler. I used to like the things." I ordered another daiquiri and brought out smokes, my mind running over the routine. I'd drive slow and give that oil a chance to soak in, then apply the pump and find out how much had really gone up in the fire and whether or not she'd done any reading before she put the torch to the evidence. Our drinks came and I paid the tab.

"To the new life," Sandy said. "May it start soon."

"New life," I echoed. We sipped the cold liquor and I thought some more about Sandy Engle. It was obvious that she'd tired of George rather quickly, probably had mistaken an infatuation for the real McCoy in the first place. He may have had the charm of an older man, but they were sadly mismated. He'd won back lost ground by being considerate during her supposed illness—now, that business exposed, she loathed the thought of him.

But he had been murdered and someone was a killer. Idly, I played with the idea that Sandy Engle had somehow found out about these things before tonight, knew George had consigned her to exile needlessly and for his own selfish motives. The concept certainly put her into line as a strong candidate for Toland's list. I wondered if—and yet I had been quite sure that the news our talkative doctor had given her had really been that.

Then she said it again. "Oooo, Marty!"

Her glass was almost empty but the reaction had been a little fast for a jigger of whiskey. Wait a second, I told myself. Sandy has switched.

"What in the hell is a whiskey cobbler?" I asked.

"One drink, Marty. Thats all little Sandy had—one drink. You said I could have one drink, Marty." She said it gleefully, like a child who has tricked an adult. The waitress was clearing away the booth behind us. She straightened up long enough to answer my question.

"Cracked ice, a bit of sugar, orange slices for decoration—that and a glass of whiskey."

By the time I squired Sandy to the car she'd given out with a couple more "Oooo, Marty's" and when I closed the door after her and went around to my side she had scooted so far to the left I had to squeeze myself in. Good Lord, I thought, if she's warped out of shape when we get back to the house it's going to be one hell of a job keeping her quiet! I opened a windwing and channeled a stream of cool night air over her face. She pressed tighter against me and didn't bother with the footsie—we teed off on a game of kneesies. Now I'm just as human as the next guy and I've never had the kind of trouble George Engle was plagued with, but there are ethics about little girls who have been nipping out of the bottle. You're pretty far down that road if you have to ply a babe with strong drink to set the mood. My campaign of the evening was going to be short and direct—play along until I got a little information, but that's all I wanted to get.

"Baby, we're really going places, you and me. We've discovered a lot of things tonight while Sheriff Toland is sitting around on his duff. Right? And I think there's more the good sheriff has missed. An envelope or two that didn't get into the fire? If we're going to be partners you wouldn't hold out on me, I hope."

"Oooo, par'ner. Put your arm around little Sanny."

That left one hand on the wheel. "And you read a few of those dossiers?"

"Ol' par'ner wants some envelopes," she giggled. "Ol' par'ner can't find any envelopes. Ol' sheriff can't either. Jus' little Sanny." She giggled again and turned sideways to give me the benefit of a gentle pressure that was all

feminine but sex was fast losing to that loggy limbo an
overdose of whiskey will bring. There's a thin band, a
zone of time when a rosy glow and a playful attitude follow the right amount of alky but on the other side the
senses are dulled and the drive gone. The barhop had
said a cobbler was a little of this and that built around a
glass of whiskey, not a jigger. Too much and too fast.
My cute brunette had been right on the edge before she
downed her cobbler and unless I missed badly she
wouldn't be making much sense before long. I wheeled
the Caddy over on the shoulder and braked to a stop.

"Oooo, Marty! You bad boy." She said it willingly,
but didn't contribute much in the way of fire. I figured
we'd be able to handle it.

"You tell ol' Marty about the envelopes, Sandy, baby."

"Not fair. Defin'ly not fair. George was a stinker—a
bad ol' stinker and I burned his papers."

"But you were a sharp little cookie," I prompted gently. "A smart little girl and you looked through some of
'em first."

"No time, ol' par'ner. But little Sanny's got 'em put
away. A smart little par'ner you got, Marty boy ol' par'-
ner."

"You tell Marty boy where. You just whisper in ol'
Marty's ear, Sanny girl," I urged and tightened my arms
around her.

"Defini'ly not fair," she repeated thickly. "All but one
has to be burned. Sanny'll read 'em all and find out
which one to keep for sheriff Tolan'—then a big ol' bon-
fire. Jus' one. One to give—"

She was slipping off fast and I cut in with "How many,
Sandy girl? How many have you got and where are
they?"

"Jus' not fair, ol' Marty, jus'—" She went a little limp
then and I eased her back toward the corner of the seat

and slipped back under the wheel. We pulled out on the road again, driving slowly, because I hoped she'd snap out of it by the time we rolled up to the estate. I needed some more information and she'd stashed some of the evidence away. I wanted to be among those who saw it first and to do that would mean get her around enough to talk some more. Then another idea hit me. Toland had searched the room and his clerk had gone over Sandy's person; a limited number of possibilities remained. I sifted then carefully for a few miles, then put my foot down on the gas and let the big hack race ahead.

Now I couldn't get Sandy home fast enough because I wasn't going to need much help locating her treasure and it would be a damn sight easier to get her in quietly if she was feeling no pain. We sped through the night and when the gravel was under our wheels and we started up, I cut the speed and doused the headlights. Nearing the estate, I dropped the hydromatic into low, let up the gas, and eased gently and quietly around a few bends and onto the parking apron, then cut the ignition. Sandy rested against the door on her side. I opened it carefully and caught her shoulders sliding out, then put an arm under her knees, lifted her clear, working the car door into place with an elbow, bumped it shut with my fanny, and started toward the house.

Moving quietly, I managed the outside door and made it almost down the hallway, but before I got to her room the phone in the main part started ringing. I faltered, then realizing I couldn't get it off the hook before someone else was awakened, I hurriedly carried Sandy into her room, put a heel to the door behind me, heard it click, and lugged the girl to her bed. For a second I hesitated, then decided that taking off her shoes was about standard operating procedure. That and folding part of the bedspread over her would complete my responsibility, but when I slipped off one high heeled shoe she stirred, then raised up and put an arm around my neck.

"Easy, baby," I whispered. "Let's you be a good little girl and hop into bed. Marty will see you in the morning. Okay?"

She went into that "Oooo, Marty!" routine again, her other arm getting into the act and it took a few moments to untangle things. It was a little like releasing yourself from the clutch of someone you're trying to pull out of the water and when I freed myself and backed off she giggled and said, "Marty, you bad, bad boy. What in the worl' are you doin' in little ol' Sanny's room?"

"That's a good question, Bowman. Care to answer the lady?"

I whipped around and stared at Bob Widdle standing in the door. "Phone call for you. I said I'd go fetch you but you weren't tucked away in your own bed, so I made the rounds. Heard you two talking in here so I opened the door."

The phone would stall it for a few minutes, give me time to think. I said, "I'll answer the call, Widdle, and be right back. We'll straighten this out in a jiffy when I return."

"I'll go along and wait for you, Bowman. Mrs. Engle would probably like to get some sleep." He fell in behind me and we went down the hall.

Fifteen

"MR. BOWMAN?" the operator asked. I said it was. "Los Angeles calling. Go ahead please."

"Marty? Fred."

"Good to hear you, boy," I said. "What have you uncovered on that end?"

"Nothing yet. Got the wires warmed up though—should have the local stuff tomorrow and the rest later in the week. Dammit, Gregory's fit to be tied. He figured this for a straight glamor assignment—not big enough to rate a regular operator. That's why he picked you. What's new with Engle?"

"He's still dead," I said wearily. "Didn't you think he would be?"

"No time for jokes, Marty. Gregory is wound up like an eight day clock. He's—"

"Leave us remember," I cut in, "that he gambled and he lost. It's that simple. He figured I was coming up here to sun myself in someone's plunge; just a little game of funsies while he rolled up a fat fee, but somebody wanted to play for keeps. So nothing could worry me less than what Gregory thinks."

"I know how you feel, kid. The way I read the afternoon edition you're in a hell of a spot."

"You couldn't be more right."

"Well, I called to tell you we're running wide open and not to worry. We'll get you cleared before long—I just wanted you to know."

"Thanks, Fred," I said. There wasn't any use telling him that if he'd stayed in bed and kept his hands off the phone I'd have gotten the Engle woman put away and back to my own room unseen. Instead I asked about Martha and Tim and how they were enjoying the beach. He said fine and good-by and hung up, but I stood there with the silent phone in my hand and tried to figure a line that Widdle would swallow.

Finally I mumbled an "Uh-huh, I'll do that," and dropped the phone back on the cradle. "Widdle, you wanted to know what I was doing in Mrs. Engle's room. Well, there's no use kidding you. We had a little date—went into town for light refreshments. She took one or two over the limit. You can—"

"You weren't to leave, Bowman. Toland's orders were—"

"Toland ordered," I cut in, "that we weren't to skip out so's he'd have to hunt for us. That was yesterday. Tonight he said he didn't want you to hear any cars going down the driveway. Mrs. Engle and I are clear on both counts. I started to tell you that you can check if you like; the Cadillac will still be warm out there. Me, I'm hitting the sack. I'm bushed."

"I'll bet you are, Bowman," Widdle said, his voice a mixture of sourness and envy.

"Why, Robert Widdle!" I said in mock surprise. "Someone should take a scrub brush to that mind of yours."

Trekking back to my room, I turned on the lights, put an ear to the door, and listened. The muffled sounds of Widdle's footsteps followed my path and stopped just outside. Grinning, I whistled my way back and forth across the room a time or two, made a sound effects production out of brushing my teeth, then flushed the john, snapped off the lights and bounced the bed a little. Barefooted I crept back to the door and a bit later Widdle's stealthy footsteps receded down the hall. I wiggled tired toes back into my shoes, let myself out the back way, hurried around to the terrace and down toward the pool.

There couldn't be many places. Sandy had brought those papers out with her—there wasn't any other way. Toland went over the room. But Sandy Engle hadn't been caught with the envelopes so there had to be a plant. Out here. I found the blanket she had asked for and later folded up. It was on a deck chair near where she'd dropped it and I shook it out, then turned it over to be sure nothing was pinned to the other side. No luck.

The shaded patio swing. She had sobbed considerably while stretched out under her blanket. She could have been working those papers out of sight under the pad. I lifted it, didn't see anything, then flopped the pad onto the grass and felt down behind the canvas back of the swing. No dice. Then I bent over the pad itself and worked along the seams. There was a slit in the canvas —short, maybe six inches—and it was more a tear like you'd make with a nail file or such. I slid a hand in and felt for the envelopes.

Nothing doing. Another two minutes of probing yielded nothing. I shoved the pad back in place and sat down. No use looking for another hiding place—the torn edge of the cloth showed new white threads; obviously the cut was made for the envelopes. Someone had aced me.

It was dark along the back walk. Very cautiously I went to each door in turn, my ear pressed hard against the thin part of the paneling as I strained for small sounds within. Cronk breathed rhythmically, steadily. I checked for several minutes. Elsa Doyle made no sound in her breathing, but waiting patiently, I heard the slight whisper of the sheets as she turned in bed.

I went on. It took most of a half hour to cover the guests and it was a half hour down the drain. Not a thing. I began to wonder about Kate and whether or not she had seen anyone in the vicinity of the pool during the evening. She had been there, diving for our boy Widdle, when I left and, after all, I had mentioned seeing her later.

Well, it was later all right, for sure—about twelve-thirty. I tapped softly on her door anyway. On the second round the window nearest the door slid up a scant two inches.

"Who's there?" Her whispered voice sounded low and clear and good to me.

"Marty. Later than I'd planned, but how's for a word or two. There have been developments, Kate."

The window closed silently and the door lock ticked

off a muffled click. I turned the knob carefully, kept it tight against the tumbler as I came through, and eased it shut. Kate pulled the blinds down and we risked the flare of a lighter, then sat on the bed and smoked as we brought each other up to date on the turn of events. Widdle had stayed glued to his deck chair, Kate told me with a smile, and she had listened for the sound of her car but heard not a thing. Our only mark in passing was, she thought, a barely visible cloud of dust that rose here and there along the lower road but even this was almost lost in the evening twilight. When we were safely on our way she had showered and slipped into a robe, and had spent the balance of her time reading in bed, then snapped off the light and gone to sleep. At eleven.

"Good girl, Kate. And you'll be glad to know that your work wasn't wasted. We found that Sandy, to use the doc's phrase, 'hasn't at present, and never has had spots or shadows on the lung.' She's clear."

"Marty, that must mean—"

"Yeah, it means a lot," I said. She was close to me now and I captured her hand. It wasn't exactly a major struggle and I felt her move slightly toward me. I laced fingers with her and said, "There's a twist to this deal we didn't know about until tonight." I told her about the X-rays and Sandy's reaction and how she reverted to what she must have been. There are some things you don't tell one lady about another, though, and I was careful to tread lightly past Sandy Engle's game of footsie and the rest. Instead I mentioned she had been holding out on us some way.

"We can find out in the morning, Marty," Kate whispered. "We'll see her when she's slept it off a while, and she'll let us help her. I'm sure she will."

"We'll try, Kate." I blew smoke rings and weighed how much more I should tell. So far I hadn't mentioned my forage through that lounge pad outside. And there didn't seem to be any good reason for doing it now—we could let Sandy Engle give us her version of that later.

"Uh, Marty," Kate's voice said that there was an amused smile on her face but in the darkness I couldn't see, "you must have put up quite a battle for your honor tonight. Or did you?"

"Now, baby," I laughed, "you—"

"I used to know Sandy Engle pretty well, Marty. Before, I mean, and if George hasn't been—well, two years—"

"Katy, my girl," I cut in, "you are going to have to keep that pretty nose of yours out of other people's lives." Then I pulled her to me and kissed her hard on the mouth. Casually at first, but halfway through it began to develop into something strictly for keeps, something warm and tight and breathless and even a bit shaky. Being noble once in an evening is about all you can expect from a man and I'd taken care of that back on the road from Lancaster. This was definitely different.

It was after two when I reached down and swept my hand in a semicircle over the floor to locate my shoes. No luck, and I had to kneel and make a search. Under the fringe of bedspread hanging down my hand touched a shoe all right but it wasn't one I could have squeezed into. It was a high-heeled, open-toe pump and it was wet. I froze momentarily—Kate Weston had said she spent the night reading in her bed. Carefully I ran my fingers over the tiny shoe. Grass clippings, also wet. Those pumps had been out for some time and could hardly have beaten me into this room by long. They sure as hell hadn't been here since evening.

"Something wrong, Marty?"

"No." I found my footwear, kissed her good night, and a few minutes later I sat on the bed in my own room,

a cigarette in my hand, wondering about Kate Weston
and her dew-soaked shoes and why she had lied to me.
me. Now where in hell had she been?

Sixteen

IT'S HARD to push something like that out of your mind.
You get to believing a woman, sure she's leveling with
you, and the awakening slaps you in the face with all the
force of a nine-foot breaker. After a while I got restless
and got up for a tour of the grounds and a little air.

Around the back walk and past the end of the building, then down toward the pool. It was almost empty
now, the shallow water swirling through the sunken
chrome drain cap in a great vortex. Across from me the
silent Philippino laid out his hose and prepared to wash
down the sides and bottom. For a fleeting moment my
eye fastened on him as he bent over his gear and I tried
to visualize him and his rarely seen wife as having a
hand in this, then gave it up. Seeing the stoic way he
went about his appointed tasks, I was sure that, unless it
had been written into his list of duties, he could hardly
have been involved. No way of being sure, of course, but
a man has to play the percentages.

Turning away, I went across the terrace and through
to the snack bar. Coffee, steaming hot with a half spoon
of sugar to take the edge off, and nothing to eat. I smoked
and waited for the coffee to cool a bit, then looked up as
the door opened on the other side and Bob Widdle came
in.

"Out late for a growing boy, aren't you, Widdle?" I
asked soberly.

"Just sitting here reading. I heard you coming and

stepped through the door and waited to see what you were up to, Bowman."

"The eye that never sleeps—you're going to be a real detective before long. All you need is one of those double-billed caps. Damn handy, Widdle. Keeps people from telling whether you're coming or going."

Widdle didn't bat an eye. "You," he pointed out, "seem to be coming and going pretty often, Bowman. I thought you just went to bed."

"Guess I broke training, coach. Couldn't sleep." He watched while I sipped the coffee, then went back to his magazine. Another one of those with a modern Samson flexing improbable biceps on the cover, and I thought idly that if he read much more of that stuff he'd be getting muscles in his teeth. I walked toward the door and said, "Going along to tuck me in, coach?"

He gave me a blank look and I went out and down the hall and shucked out of my clothes. I didn't even listen to see if Widdle had followed me. It wasn't important, somehow. Nothing seemed important except that Bowman had been so wrong about a blonde named Weston. I fell asleep trying to figure where she could have been that was so secretive that she had to peddle me a big greasy line about spending the evening with a good book.

Sunday morning started out in low gear and jumped to high in a hurry. It began with low clouds that skimmed the tops of the hills behind us and merged with gray vapor rising out of the upper storage tank. I looked out the back window for several minutes while collecting my thoughts from yesterday, then brushed my teeth, showered and shaved, combed, slipped into tan slacks and a green sport shirt and headed for breakfast. Bob Widdle, dark rings bearing silent witness that he had kept the night vigil and perhaps plowed through considerable

material on the care and maintainance of the human car-
cass, was just finishing his coffee. The only other member on hand was Cronk, and I gave out with a cheery,
"Good morning." It reaped a modest harvest; a curt
nod from Widdle and a grunt that could have been anything from, "Hello," to, "Go to hell," from Cronk. It was
fairly evident that our conversation would be something
less than sparkling and it hardly seemed worth the effort.
I started on grapefruit and, when Widdle got up to leave,
I tossed back that curt nod he had loaned me. Cronk
was still at the table when I polished off my short stack,
finished the coffee, and went in search of Kate.

She wasn't in her room but I found her reading by the
pool, her smooth brown curves displayed in a filmy light
blue nylon creation that probably cost—was very
nice looking indeed. I made the last part of that observation out loud.

"Thanks, Marty. You've had breakfast?" I told her
I had and asked if she was ready to make that social call
on Sandy Engle. "I stopped by a few minutes ago, Marty.
She isn't up, or at least she didn't answer. We'd better
wait a while, I think."

"In comfort," I said, and dropped on a nearby lounge.
It was refreshing to know we weren't going into
any downcast-eyes and you-won't-respect-me-any-more
routine. She folded the paper and we chatted about this
and that; verbal sparring until it got around to those
envelopes again. She hadn't the least doubt that we'd be
able to talk Sandy Engle into making it a three-way partnership, a thing I wasn't at all sure of, but there was nothing to be gained in saying so. I didn't mention that it was
highly unlikely that Sandy could produce them anyway now—that someone had raided the hiding place and
carried off the loot. Or did she already know that? Maybe
that dew on those tiny shoes of hers had been acquired

while Kate was digging out those white envelopes. Then she pointed up the walk behind me.

"Company, Marty."

Mrs. Pilcher was coming toward the pool, her fat fanny encased in a pink knitted suit, the like of which people of her beam shouldn't fool with in any way. Probably she had passed breakfast, a minor concession to that increasing weight, but she wasn't coming out to chat with us. We might have been part of the scenery, almost, because we rated no more than a cool glance. We kept our voices low enough not to bother her with our ideas and she must have gotten bored with the silence because she got up again, wandered around the pool to the far side, and went through the opening in the cypress and down the winding path of flagstone. About three minutes later we heard the scream.

I stared at Kate, then jumped to my feet and raced around the edge of the plunge and down the walk. At the second concrete park bench, the one against the jacaranda tree, I saw them—the still screaming Mrs. Pilcher and, on the bench, her head tossed back against the tree, Sandy Engle. But it wasn't just a restful pose. Even as I sprinted toward them I caught the odd way her head had angled off and then the black wire ends sticking out behind the tree trunk.

I stopped, like you do while your mind takes in the picture in one quick flash. An old wire coat hanger had been straightened out, then slipped around her neck and the trunk of that jacaranda, pulled tight, hauling her slender white neck tight against the tree just above the top of the bench, and given a few hasty turns to keep it in place. Neat and sweet—no blood, no sound, no chance to work free. She must have—suddenly I scooted around behind the bench, grabbed the wire, whipped the ends around until the loop fell free, and vaulted over in time to ease Sandy Engle down to a horizontal position. It was time for a king-sized yell and the name that flashed to mind was Widdle. I bellowed it once at the top of my lungs, just as Kate Weston came in sight, then bent to look at Sandy.

She was already cold, not breathing of course, and when I lifted an eyelid there was no reaction, no change in the size of the pupil. No use to feel for a pulse, but I did it. I did it knowing that she would be far past any help —gone—irrevocably consigned to join George Engle in whatever was slated to follow their brief stay on earth. I bit my lip and shook my head. Poor Sandy. She had been one of those who really love the gay and vibrant way of living but an eccentric husband had deprived her of two full years of that life. Then last night, with a beach boy named Bowman, she'd recaptured a small part of her world, found the key and opened the door leading back to the bright brittle world she had lost. And for how long?

A few hours. From the half dazed moment when the doctor said she had never really been sick, to the first bar, then a short ride in Kate's big car and another drink and then the picture faded for a time. How long had she slept and who had gotten her out here? A few hours' reprieve. Then her tomorrows snuffed out by a black wire drawn tight behind a jacaranda tree. I straightened and looked down at her. At least one thing was settled—she didn't have to sit quietly and watch others enjoy the full life any more. She was past that now.

Vaguely I was aware that reinforcements had arrived, that Widdle was standing beside me, his mouth hanging open as he stared down at Sandy Engle.

"Better send for the boss," I reminded him gently.

He looked at me, then decided on another errand boy, probably because Bob Widdle had an idea that Bowman should be where he could be kept an eye on. At a word from him, Cronk worked his pudgy rump into a dog-trot toward the house. Widdle held his arms out and backed a few feet.

"Stay clear of her. Nobody touches her until Mr. Toland gets here."

Nobody wanted to.

It was as gruesome a half hour as I've put in lately, and I guessed that the others didn't enjoy it much, either. We stood in threes, Cronk joining his fat friends when he puffed back into our midst and Kate and Elsa flanking a very worried boy named Bowman—at that moment I might have been born only yesterday.

After the passing of about a hundred thousand years, Sheriff Toland steamed on the scene. He looked at Sandy Engle, then at us. The wire still hung loosely across her shoulders. Toland bent over it, but didn't touch it.

"It's been bent into a pretty big loop," he said to no one in particular.

I said, more to make sure I was there than for any other reason, "It was slipped on from behind the tree, I think. I found it twisted together back of the jacaranda trunk—neck and tree together."

"Who loosened it?" Toland looked at me and I looked back at him. He didn't have to repeat the question. "Now, son, don't tell me you dug in and mussed up the body and got your prints all over everything again. Not another one of these where I got to remember you tried to help."

"Suppose," I said, "you had found her. She might have been there two minutes. Or half a minute. Anyway she looked like hell. So I just stand there and watch her die while you drive up from Newhall? Be reasonable, Toland."

"I'm trying to be reasonable, Bowman," Toland said firmly. "So you're not a shamus—so you're here on false pretenses. Have you got to louse things up? All I want is to get to the bottom of this. The way it's going, though,

I haven't really got any problem. All I got to do is wait until there's only one of you left up here, then cart him off for killing the others. Right, Bowman?"

I had nothing to say to that. He turned to his understudy. "Widdle, you phone the coroner's office and tell him we've got some Sunday work that won't wait. Then pick up a blanket and get back here—we'll see how far we can go with this. You've been riding herd on these people and you should be here when they tell me where they've been; it'll keep 'em from forgetting things a little." Widdle went up the flagstones on the double and Toland had another look at Sandy Engle. He stood up again, put a tired hand to his hat, then pulled the hat off and held it in his big brown fist as he walked back to look at the jacaranda.

"Marks of the wire here," he pointed out, mostly to himself. "Not too deep, though. And I guess the source of that wire would have been available to everyone. Just an old coat hanger you'd find in any closet."

No one had any appropriate comments to make, and in due time Widdle returned.

Toland turned to me. "I guess you found her, eh, Bowman?"

"No. Not this time, Sheriff. It was Mrs. Pilcher."

The sheriff raised a questioning eyebrow in her direction and she explained that she'd been strolling down the path and come onto this. She screamed and Mr. Bowman came dashing to the rescue. She hadn't touched a thing.

"I know, ma'm. It's Bowman whose fingers get into things. Now how many of you have seen Mrs. Engle this morning? Before breakfast, say, or just after?" He didn't get any response so he jumped back to last night. "What about after dinner? She around then?"

A damned fast worker, I thought. He caught most of us staring.

"Sandy has been staying in her room since—since you

were here last," Kate said quietly. "Understandably, she didn't want to be with anyone after you found out about—" But I didn't hear the rest of Kate's explanation. I was watching Bob Widdle's face and he was watching mine. There wasn't anything to do but take a big breath and dive in.

"Toland," I cut in. "I know it looks like hell, but I'm afraid you'll have to put me down for seeing her last. Except for whoever got her out here and wound that wire around her throat, I mean. I was with Sandy Engle last night. From evening until midnight, and we even sneaked off bounds for a while. We did have, though, one hell of a good reason."

"That would be a good place to start, son—the reason."

I gave it to him from the time I began to guess that Sandy was being kidded about her illness right on through until we came home and I parked her in her bed. I even gave Widdle a credit line for surprising us. Kate had heard most of it, of course, but the redhead was giving me an appraising eye before I finished and so were some of the others.

Elsa Doyle was watchful, waiting for developments. Dan Pilcher was frankly skeptical and didn't mind its showing. He'd dredged up an old-fashioned match to chew on and it moved up and down between his teeth as he said, "I sure hope you don't see me last one of these nights. Seems like every time somebody's with you late in the evening—" He cut it off when Toland gave him a sharp look but the smirk built around the match lingered on.

"And then you went in and crawled between the sheets, Bowman. That right?" Toland prompted.

"Yes, and no, Sheriff." I fumbled for my smokes and took a little time lighting one. There was going to have to be a slight variation here to account for the time I'd been with Kate. Neither hell nor high water was going to bring that to light. I blew a smoke ring and said, "Naturally I couldn't sleep, Toland, because—"

"You mean thinking about this girl wired to the tree out here?" Cronk asked wickedly. "How does Toland know you didn't slip back to her room, bring her out along the path to this bench, and tighten that coat hanger around her, Bowman?"

"You'd better examine her, Doctor," I said with mock sincerity. "She had a bad heart, no doubt."

"Would anyone mind if I ran things for a while?" Toland put in firmly. "You went to bed around midnight, Bowman? Nobody can swear to that, but you say it's true."

"Well—" I caught myself. I almost suggested he ask Widdle. "No. I left Widdle after my phone call but of course he doesn't know that I came back to my room."

"He did. I was by shortly afterwards and heard him in there," Widdle said.

"Uh-huh. And when did this insomnia set in, Bowman?"

"About two, or a few minutes after. I walked around the pool once, then into the snack bar for coffee. Widdle was still up."

Bob nodded to Toland. "Two-sixteen. That's when he came in and got the coffee. He left at two-twenty-three."

"He came in at two-sixteen," Toland observed dryly. "You haven't any way of knowing when he left his room, Bob."

"That's right," Widdle admitted. "From about twelve-thirty until he came in no one saw him. An hour and a half or better."

"Uh-huh. Who else was up last night? You see anyone other than Bowman around, Bob?" He got a negative shake of the head from Widdle, then turned back to the rest of us. "How about it?"

No one answered. I forced myself not to look at Kate Weston, just listened to what she'd say. But she said nothing. I whistled softly.

It didn't improve any in the next little while. Toland questioned everyone in detail but nothing more worth noting was tossed into the pot. When the coroner brought his stretcher down the path and they took Sandy away we followed along up to the house.

The sun was high overhead but food was out of the question and Toland worked ahead, getting everyone fixed as to what time they corked off and who saw who last. I gave it a careful ear because anything I could pick up would help. Nothing could hurt—I was already the prime nominee. When Widdle asked about Kate's time schedule she gave it to him just the way I heard it last night. In her room all evening after that brief swim—a book and then to bed. Not out. When the sheriff had it all down he turned to Widdle.

"This time no one leaves, Bob. For any reason." Then turning to us: "I don't want anyone running around the grounds. Stay in the house or on the front terrace. Got that? Anything I don't need up here is someone else getting it. I'm going to take a run into Lancaster to see those people you dealt with last night, Bowman, and by God they'd better go along with the story you're telling."

Nobody said anything as he went out. I looked at Kate and shook my head.

"I'm sorry," she breathed softly, "to've gotten you into such a mess. I'm—"

"Take it easy, kid," I said. "We'll work something out. We'll have to. Let's take a stroll—at least the terrace is ours."

She linked an arm through mine and fell into step, her high heels ticking along the stone, her fingers sliding down my arm and lacing with my hand.

But she hadn't mentioned being out last night—neither to me nor to Toland. It wasn't anything new, I told myself. Beautiful women have been making suckers out of guys for a long time now. Marty Bowman was just one of a lineage that stretched back a long way. No, it wasn't anything new but it was damn uncomfortable, enough so that a man ought to try to do something about it.

Seventeen

WE STOOD and watched a breeze whip tiny ripples across the water. Now and then I felt the warm pressure of Kate's fingers in mine and gave a quick return. But I had already detached her from the oneness we had known last night—I was working alone from here in. We walked leisurely around the oval of the pool, but when we came near the opening in the cypress our names echoed down to us. Bob Widdle stood by the front door of the house and gestured us away from the path.

"The human bloodhound," I said smiling. "If we want peace and quiet we'll have to settle right here someplace."

Kate stopped by the lawn swing. We sat down, and I gave us a gentle push. The swing drifted in smooth easy motion, the light nylon of Kate's blue dress stirring in the air currents.

"Why Sandy, Marty?" she asked suddenly. "George was engaged in a dangerous business and his death is understandable. But why Sandy?"

"I wish I knew," I said sadly. But I lied—because I did know. I was quite sure, in fact, but I no longer felt under an obligation to tell Kate Weston. I hadn't been hired to solve a murder—much less two—and what had happened between us last night had to stand on its own. It had either been right or it hadn't—and a lie had no place in it.

George's murder was planned; Sandy's was a "must" brought about by a sheaf of white paper—those missing envelopes and the old game of kill once more. It was that simple.

"Marty, let's take them one by one and see where they fit in the puzzle," Kate suggested. "We could run through the list and see what the evidence is against each and who looks like the guilty one."

"Let's not settle on the one who looks most likely," I said pointedly.

"I know, Marty, and I'm sorry. But we're both sure neither of us could have done this—this thing. So knowing that, we could work together, narrow down the field—"

I listened and put in my nickel's worth every little while, but I didn't contribute anything new. From here on if anything looked hot, Marty Bowman was strictly for himself, but I went along with her on the surface. She dug into Cronk first and went through how he wanted to let well enough alone when George was pulled out of the water and how he would surely be tried for posing as an M.D. and had a lot to gain by George's death.

"Maybe he isn't too badly off after all," I said. "Look at it this way. If he'd cut someone or loused up a diagnosis and killed a patient there'd be pure hell to pay. He didn't, though. He just slipped through whoever is supposed to screen the medical profession, as far as we know. This will embarrass more people than Cronk, I'd guess, but it's even money that they'll ease him out with very little publicity and a small fine. Why should he get a sweat up now? If he didn't kill Engle he hasn't a thing to worry about that the rest of us don't—by the way, what do you think of Toland?"

"I want to stick to Cronk."

"All right—but you'll have to admit that he's done some clever broken-field running Kate. He's pretty well clear so far. After the story he handed Toland about keeping quiet so as not to scare off the killer, it's a wonder they didn't give him a deputy's badge and put him on the payroll. We'd better pass up Cronk for the time being."

She went from there to Elsa—no progress. We rounded up the entire tribe in the next few hours of course, and added almost nothing to the fund of information. About the only forward stride the entire day brought was elimination of one suspect—Sandy.

Kate and I walked a little and tried the deck chairs and walked some more and came back to the swing to spend some time just sitting. Finally she disengaged her hand and stood up, her fingers smoothing her blue dress in slow deliberation.

"Something is wrong, Marty. I'm not sure just what it is—is it last night, or something you've found out?" She said it quietly, her eyes going back and forth across my face in a half hurt, half wondering expression, making her look young—younger than she had a right to look. I walked her around to the far side of the swing where a small measure of privacy could be had.

"Look, baby," I said earnestly, "this is murder and we're right in the middle of it." I slipped both arms around her waist, locked my fingers. She leaned back against my arms and put her hands on my chest. Easy, boy, I told myself, don't let's get carried away again. I forced a smile.

"No one can say Marty Bowman is against romance, Kate, or that you aren't the girl to inspire it. But Toland has gone to Lancaster to talk to some people and when he gets back he will no longer be a man of thought. He'll be reaching for his handcuffs when he comes through that door over there, and let's not kid about it, so—"

"What will he find in Lancaster, Marty?"

There wasn't any point in holding that one fact out any longer. "He will find, when he gets as far as a certain bar, that I was there last night with Sandy Engle. In itself, not too incriminating, but there were those daiquiris I had. Weak limeade, while loading Sandy with hard drink. And what will that look like?"

"But I don't understand, Marty."

"I bribed a barkeep to fill mine with lime and water. I wanted Sandy drunk enough to talk, without getting helpless myself."

"My God," she breathed. "It'll look as though you were deliberately getting Sandy drunk so—"

"Yeah, getting her drunk so—and he won't be thinking I had sex on my mind. You see how it is, baby? All I want to do is sit here by this pool of Engle's and think. No one is going to get Bowman out of this but Bowman, and he can't do it by playing house.". .

She stood on tiptoe and kissed me full on the mouth. "Marty, you're still holding out. I know it—don't ask me how, but I feel it someplace inside and if you can't tell me, or don't think you should, that's all right too. I'm going up and rest a while. If—if you think of something that will help, let me know because I'm just as worried as you are. I wish you'd believe that."

She turned and hurried around the end of the swing and up toward the house. I stepped to one side and watched until she went running up the steps, heard the quick tap of her high heels on the cement as she crossed the porch, and saw the door close after her. Then I found a lounge pad, tossed it down on the cement near the edge of the pool and assumed the horizontal.

Toland, Bowman and Widdle and everyone else who was trying to iron this out were on the wrong track, had followed the wrong star. Motive? Who has the most to gain? It sounds good and it is good, but only if you can be sure who gained and how much. Here, it wouldn't work. Too many people had plenty to gain—the evidence had finally been destroyed, probably, and only the murderer was alive to say what it had been.

Maybe we should have settled first on the method used to kill George Engle. Toland had decided on strangulation, but I pulled Engle out of the pool and if he had shown any marks of being strangled I should have seen them. Or perhaps not, in the semi-darkness, and yet . . . well, surely a man's oxygen supply can be cut off in more ways than one. Now suppose. . . .

My fingers dipped into the warm water and I scooped up a handful, let it pour over the edge of my palm. Gas or poison would have shown up at the autopsy; Engle had neither. Suffocation, they had said. He couldn't breathe. And a dollar in his fingers, a silver dollar belonging to Bowman—yet George clutched it tightly at the moment of his death. Now how did he get it and why was it in his hand . . . in the pool? I scooped out another fistful of water, saw the ripples spread over the surface of the clear warm water, saw the huge stainless steel drain grill below suddenly dancing and distorted as the ruffled water bent the light. It settled back to its oval shape again as the water became still. Two nights ago Engle had lain down there, fifteen feet of sparkling water washing over him as he rested on the bottom. . . .

And there it was.

There it was, like the flash of a color slide thrown suddenly on a white screen—Engle down in the pool and how he died and where my dollar fitted in.

Vaguely I became conscious that a soft whistle was escaping through my lips. I guess no one knows just how the mind works, how it makes certain connections, juggles the pieces into place and into a pattern we call thought. You work on a problem for days and make no appreciable headway and suddenly you solve it, see the solution in one quick flash that, for lack of a better name, they call inspiration. And once the foundation is laid you can forge ahead with giant strides and alter and shape until the corners are rounded down and the finished result obtained. Suddenly I could almost see Engle as he had been in one of his last living moments, waving to me before going to work some more on his diving. I got up and looked around slowly, then whistled again and shoved my hands into my pockets and measured the opening in the cypress with my eye.

Death had come through that parting in the trees. Death had watched and waited, and beckoned to George Engle.

I struck a match and found my cigarettes. It was almost dark now, lights showing through the huge picture window of Engle's living room, but I wasn't hungry and if the air had cooled I didn't notice. There was much to be done and so little time. For an instant I felt the wind go out of my sails as I remembered that I still hadn't made a single stride toward finding out who had killed Engle, then felt my spirits building again, because having found the way was a large part of the battle. Now I could plan—could weigh and reject and bluff a little if need be. Now Marty Bowman was in the driver's seat.

Eighteen

HANDS DEEP in my pockets again, I began to lap the pool, my mind squirming around for a way to break through the barrier. Marty Bowman had taken the pale and lovely Sandy Engle to town last night. He had brought her home about three sheets to the gale and feeling no pain, a fact that the Sheriff was going to make much of, but. . . .

Now there were five horses in the race, five possible names to draw from and the very least I could hope for was to have something reasonably good on the fire by the time Sheriff Toland returned.

It took another hour to work out an angle, a point of departure. I went to the house, hiked around to my room by the back way and started to wash up for dinner. A shower, a change of clothes, and I went down to the big dining room where, until two days ago, George and Sandy Engle entertained insurance prospects who were willing to pay premiums on policies that were never written. Engle's man, now in a white jacket, was setting up a buffet, something light and informal for the end of a hectic day. I went on through to the snack bar, looked carefully around the room, then walked over to the assortment of trays stacked vertically in a narrow cupboard. A heavy aluminum one, about cafeteria size, caught my eye and I took it out for close examination, then slid it back, scooped up a magazine, and went back through to the living room.

Mrs. Pilcher sat heavily in the center section of Engle's fancy davenport and across the room Elsa Doyle's well turned gams extended out from a newspaper resting on her lap. I crossed over, found a seat near Elsa, then moved my chair closer as she gave me a big hello.

"A busy man these days, this Bowman," she observed with a smile. "Lots of overtime. At night, yet."

"An honest day's work for a day's pay," I said with a wink. "You ever need an eye in a hurry, keep Gregory's agency in mind."

"And get a beach boy," she taunted, then softened it with: "I could easily do a lot worse though, couldn't I?"

You don't answer that kind of a question. I changed the subject. "You haven't been among us much, Elsa, since our host got wet the other night. No pay no work? You did call it a job, I remember."

"I've been busy, too," she said, and took the smoke I offered. "I brought a script along, hoping to get some time to go over the thing. It'll be my next and it looks good—will you go to see it, Marty?"

"I hope so, Elsa," I said evenly, "but as George said, there are plenty of pitfalls for show people. It's a precarious occupation, I guess—you're up one day and down the next. At least, that was George's theory the night he introduced us."

She blew a careful cone of smoke to one side and met my eyes. "Your memory is pretty good, Marty."

"Yeah. It makes sense. Living under glass, you rise and fall by the public's whim. Good publicity or bad."

"I'm not sure I follow you, Marty. Some of that George never said, I'm sure."

"Maybe," I said blandly. "I'm just hoping your next picture'll knock 'em dead and that I'll be there to see it."

She laughed suddenly, but without too much conviction, I thought. "Marty—you sound almost ominous. You think I'm going to let this mess affect my career?"

"It would seem like a good idea not to," I said carelessly, then asked, "Have you any idea who might have put that wire around poor Sandy, Elsa?"

She said she didn't and we went from there to other things. When Pilcher came into the room and added his poundage to the load on the davenport, I excused myself and went over for a chat with Dan. Elsa gave me a smile to take along but I caught her eyes in the mirror as I crossed the room and that bright red head was strictly alert, the newspaper forgotten on her lap.

Dropping down on the end of the sofa, I gave Pilcher my best grin and said, "Well, Dan, we'll be clearing here tomorrow, maybe. You'll be glad to get away, no doubt."

"Hell, yes, Bowman. Need you ask?" His eyes darted back and forth across my face, Mrs. Pilcher added her puzzled look to the attack, and the expressions of both said they didn't quite understand what was going on, but weren't sure they liked it.

"Pretty lucky, weren't you, boy?" I said, and shook my head. "All of the literature Engle had assembled going up the flue like that. Mighty convenient, Pilcher."

He gave me a hard look, then let it fade. A sardonic smile took over. "Why, Bowman, what an imagination! As I told Toland, George and I were just good friends."

"You think the sheriff is buying that?"

"A hell of a lot I care, Bowman. He's either got to accept it or prove it isn't so."

"Except he seems to think some of the evidence wasn't burned," I said, my eyes on the tip of my cigarette. "It would certainly change things if that turned out to be true, wouldn't it? And even if the papers were burned since, if he knew what they'd said he could go to the original source and dig until he uncovered things—"

"Meaning?" Pilcher snapped.

"Never a thing, Danny, boy. That is if you're sure you're pure. How could anything hurt you?" I excused myself, got up and walked through to the dining room, and went to the buffet.

Cronk had come in and so had Kate Weston, and the Philippino passed me as he went to call the three from the other room. We made up our plates, trekked back through to the living room and sat around with our food balanced on the arms of our chairs. Widdle came through the doorway, a heaping plate in his right hand balanced by a mere cup of coffee in the left. He parked near me, set his groceries on the glass coffee table in front, and looked around the room.

"What's the word from the boss?" I asked casually.

He didn't answer, just took a bite of cold ham, carefully worked it over, then swallowed a time or two. "Bowman, it seems like you asked that same question before. You're sure on edge about when Toland comes and goes."

"Everyone here is anxious to leave," I pointed out. "I simply wondered when he'd be around."

"Nobody else seems worried," Widdle said quickly. We ate in silence for a few minutes; then Widdle said, "Later tonight, maybe. He phoned from Newhall, and if it'll make you happy, Bowman, he's been talking to a lot of people in Lancaster today. He said to tell you."

"Thanks," I said sourly. "If he's trying to keep me awake nights he's doing a pretty good job. Tell him for me, next time he calls."

It drew a grunt from Widdle. I laid in a thin ham sandwich, coffee, and a baked apple and called it a meal. Across from me Kate Weston picked uneasily at her food, then pushed the plate aside and sipped coffee, her blue eyes catching mine from time to time and then turning away. She looked incongruously like a wall flower, a little girl who was being left out of things.

Cronk was more dejected tonight than before, probably because the full impact of his washed-out career as a radiologist was setting in. He sat, his chin almost down to his chest, his eyes listless behind thick glasses and spoke to no one.

I needed more time to work out details and I could do nicely without any company. Pushing my plate and cup toward the center of the tiny glass table, I stood up, took a slow look around the room, and went toward the terrace. The door closed after me and then opened again.

"Marty." It was Kate, and I turned to wait for her. "I'd like to talk to you a second. You—"

"Sure." I turned toward the pool again when she was beside me and we walked several steps in silence.

"Marty, have you—did you figure out who killed Sandy and George? I mean if you've found out and haven't told me, I wish you would because I got you into this and we were going to work on it together, you said. That first night, or was it early morning after George died. Remember?"

"I remember," I said softly. I patted her hand, then took it gently off of my arm. "Baby, there is a lot to be said, but this isn't the moment. You trot back to the house like a good little chick and get some rest. I'll be seeing you later. Then we'll hash it over from the bottom up—but not now."

I turned away and walked down the strip of concrete and there weren't any steps going the other way. When I turned to pace around the pool I could see Kate still where I had left her. Finally she turned and went slowly toward the house. There was the silence of the water and from beyond the cypress came night sounds—wind sighed through the heavily shrubbed area bordering the flagstone path. I smoked and wandered aimlessly, and about ten trekked back to my room. I stalled the time it takes to smoke one cigarette, then went in search of Bob Widdle. I found him in the snack bar.

"Hello, Bowman," he said cautiously.

I gave him a friendly smile, then looked carefully all around. "Get ready for some music, Widdle," I said. "Bowman is turning stool pigeon. I think we're going to lose a customer or two before long. I get the feeling someone hasn't heard Toland's orders about staying on the grounds."

He eyed me suspiciously, then put his magazine down. "Not Bowman, though. He's staying close to the estate, I guess."

"He is. For sure, Widdle. I certainly can't afford to add any more to Toland's picture of me—it's black enough already. So now I've told you. It's your baby."

He looked me over again, weighing the information.

Finally he said, "Who, Bowman, when and where?"

"No idea, Widdle. But you could make sure by blocking the road. There's only one way out, unless somebody wants to hoof it." While he was thinking it over, I flipped the keys to Kate's Cad on the table. I said, "Take these and back the big wagon crosswise just below the apron. It won't be any trouble to seal off the road. You can keep the keys. Fair enough?"

He whistled lightly a moment or two, then fingered the keys as he watched me. "I'll do that, Bowman. You can come along, just to help." I said I'd be glad to and in a few minutes we had the moneybags special jammed sideways to the gravel, her big chrome bumpers within a yard of the embankment on one side and almost to the steep drop-off on the other. I got out and started toward the house but Widdle snapped the catch and opened the hood. Leaning under, he fumbled in the darkness, then went around to the other side. When he backed out he held a small part in his hand.

"Just in case you have a spare set of keys, Bowman, I'm taking the rotor out of the distributor. You can have it back if and when the Sheriff says it's all right for you to go." He paused, then added: "You see how it is, Bowman."

"Very sharp." I nodded and smiled. "Ah, there's one thing more, Widdle. It might be a good idea to round up the hands and make it clear that Toland instructed them to stay. That way, no one could claim they hadn't heard. Right?"

"I'll do that. In the living room. I'll call 'em down there now."

"Just to make sure," I approved, and didn't bother to tell him that we were talking about different things.

Back in my room, I slipped into bathing trunks, opened my grip and rummaged for Fred's stubby little .38, wrapped it up in the folds of a beach towel, pulled on a robe, and went down to stand muster for Widdle's announcement.

"You are hereby reminded," Widdle said stiffly, after he'd assembled the group, "that Sheriff Toland left orders not to leave. Each is witness that the others have heard. No one is to go farther than the house or terrace. Now go back to bed."

He turned and went toward his station in the snack bar. Cronk looked his disgust and grunted, "How many times does he have to tell us?"

I kept still and waited for an opening. Kate looked from one to another and let her eyes stop on me momentarily, then looked away. Elsa Doyle tossed in a few well chosen and indignant words but they didn't lead where I wanted to go either. I had to kick it off myself.

"Happy dreams, boys and girls," I said cheerily, "and to many more happy days here in the hills."

"Not if I can help it," Pilcher put in. "The sooner I clear out of here the better. What's more, if I never see any of Engle's guests again it'll be weeks too soon."

Which was the type of thing I'd been angling for. "You will, though. All of you will."

A feather dropping on the carpet would have made itself heard. "We're different that way, Danny boy," I went on pointedly. "I like the guests here a lot—enough to want to see you all again. If Toland gets it settled in the morning and lets us go our ways you can still depend on a visit from Marty Bowman." I worked up a sarcastic smile, spread it over the five of them, and went toward the snack bar.

Widdle looked up when I came in. "Don't you ever sleep, Bowman?"

"And you, Widdle?"

"A wink here and there. Now what the hell are you doing?"

"Hungry," I said shortly. I built a pair of sandwiches,

drew a mug of steaming coffee, spilled a bit of sugar into it, pulled out and loaded the heavy aluminum tray, and went down to the pool. I laid my towel on a deck chair and set the food down, then touched a foot to the water. Already the coolness of the day was getting to it, a fact which didn't reduce its attractiveness as far as I was concerned. I took a couple from the diving board, swam a few lengths and crawled out for coffee and a sandwich.

And I listened. Sitting with my back to the water, I listened and thought about how things had been the night George Engle died. A planned murder, coldly and carefully done, but it wasn't that way with Sandy Engle. Panic showed through when Sandy was killed. Panic and the haste that follows in its wake, and with a little luck we could have someone on edge at the moment. Someone besides Bowman, that is, because I sure as hell couldn't claim to be cool and collected. I took my time with the first sandwich, sipped coffee, and then swam another dozen lazy lengths of the plunge. Pulling myself out on the deep end, I went back to finish my lunch. Face toward the house and path, the direction down which trouble would most likely come, I sat and sipped the now almost cold coffee.

And then, just barely audible behind me, there was a small splash in the pool.

The cup froze in my hand and I made myself stay glued to the deck chair against the desire to jump and run through the wall of cypress. To do that would prove nothing, would scatter and destroy the plans I'd put together. You can't convict anyone for tossing something into a swimming pool. I waited several minutes, then set the coffee cup down on the concrete and put the plate beside it. Turning toward the pool, I looked at the bottom and, shining there, clearly seen by the lights glowing below water line, was a cigarette lighter. Chrome or silver, its detail still slightly distorted by the ripples not yet dead on the surface of the water.

I took a deep breath, grabbed the heavy aluminum tray, and dove toward the cigarette lighter.

Nineteen

THE COOL WATER closed over me, the tray slid through edgewise like the diving planes of a sub and I kicked a time or two as I went down. Straightening out near the bottom, I headed for the cigarette lighter, but when the oval stainless steel drain grill was below the tray, a mighty downward current of water pulled the aluminum tray to the bottom and slammed it tight against the grill. I pried at the rim of the serving tray, knowing as I worked that I would never budge it, that a force of almost half a ton had clamped it over the drain. George Engle had seen a silver dollar on the bottom of the pool, a silver dollar that shouldn't have been there, and when he knifed down through fifteen feet of water that drain was open and Engle was pinned to its mouth. It had to be that way.

I shoved upwards from the tile bottom, broke surface and hauled myself out, slid a hand in to Fred's gun, with the towel still wrapped around it. I ran around the pool toward the opening in the cypress. Down by the valve—there I would find the answer. I hurried along the flag-stones, then cut off into the shrubbery and slowed to a careful walk. They would have to wait by the valve, a hand on the heavy steel crank, and listen to the water draining out of the pool. Marty Bowman was supposed to be stuck to the bottom back there, sucked down and unable to free himself. And like the first class job they did on Engle, the repeat performance would involve waiting a few minutes. Three, say, or maybe even five minutes after the slowing of the flow told them that their man was in the trap. Then turn the steel crank and close the valve and wait. A small amount of water was bound to leak past the human obstruction caught against the grill, and when enough flowed through to fill the pipe between valve and the body, the pressure would be equalized and the victim free—no longer pressed tight against the drain.

Still, just enough had gone wrong with Engle's execution to make it murder instead of the accidental drowning it was supposed to be. Engle had suffocated, instead of drowning, and I knew why.

Nearing the shut-off valve, I moved slowly, slipped from bush to bush as I closed. Working carefully, I made the fringe lining the cleared area and put enough head up for a look around. A shaft of moonlight caught the steel valve and there was no one near it, the crank handle was gone. Peering through the semi-darkness, I checked as best I could but there was no sign of anyone, no sound. Then a quick movement behind me, the sudden whisper of cloth as I tried to turn, tried to stand up. The heavy *wump* and momentary flash of pain surging through my head—then that long fall through black silence, the end of thought and feeling. . . .

Slowly the bush beside me took shape and my fingers closed on a handful of grass and dew. I closed my eyes and lay for several seconds more, the grass wet and cold against my bare skin, my mind bringing back the pieces and putting me in the world of reality. Opening both eyes again, I looked toward the valve. Fred's shiny .38 lay on the dew-wet steel pipe of the outflow and beside it, her red hair almost black in the half-light, stood Elsa Doyle.

I started to roll over but the redhead put a hand on the gun beside her.

"Hold it, Marty. Just stay put, please." I didn't like the sound of her voice. There was a lostness and a flatness in her tone that was somehow deadly on the night air. I took a quick breath and tried to jar her out of the dream.

"Look, baby, this won't get you any place. We're at the end of the trail—finished. You tossed my buck in the pool and sucked George Engle tight to the grill. He died there, and when you found those papers and knew Sandy had had a chance at them, you slipped a wire around her neck. That's murder, baby—no turning back, no dream to wake from, no director to yell 'cut' and end the scene on a coffee break. Hell, kid—this was for real. They're dead, Sandy and George, and your luck has petered out."

"But only you know, Marty. Only you." She didn't say it menacingly or with any particular anger.

I swallowed a couple of times, my hands tensing, pressing the wet grass. If she started to use the gun, I had to try something. Near the girl's feet I saw the handle from the valve. She must have used it to knock me out—the pain in my head was beginning to register now. Hazily I tried to figure the vagueness of her voice, tried to get her mind fully with me.

"You saw me use the tray, Elsa?"

"No. But there was the sound of the metal when the water shut off. I had the thing open, the pool draining, and then there was the clinking noise and I knew it couldn't have been you that hit the drain cap."

"You slipped that steel handle off, then, and went back along the path?"

The redhead nodded silently, but I hadn't gained an inch. Her answer and that detached way she spoke both told me that I was only dealing with the top of her mind, and that underneath was something entirely apart from the words she uttered. I tried again, attempted to focus her thoughts with mine.

"You found the papers Sandy hid. In the lounge pad, I guess?"

"In the lounge pad, Marty. I had the jump on you—I was instantly worried about her keeping some of the evidence out. I watched and thought about it, and that night I found them there."

"So that meant Sandy had to go, too, Elsa?"

"She might have read them. I was already in too deep. I stayed outside most of the night when you were gone with her, Marty. When the car came back I waited under her window and heard Widdle catch you putting her to bed, heard you two go back down to the snack bar. Then I went back to my room and thought about the path and the jacaranda. It was no trouble to talk her into going down the walk to wait for me. . . ."

She had killed twice, but she was still an amateur. Before she could murder a third time, she had to talk about the first two, just to convince herself that the third killing was necessary. Now she started to move, her hand still close to the gun beside her. The moment had come— now she had told me . . . now I had to die.

I tried to keep her talking. "And now, Elsa? Murder's never easy—you found that out the first time, with Engle. He was supposed to drown, wasn't he? I'll bet you never figured the odds of his being sucked into that sunken drain face first, so that instead of drowning he suffocated. That made it murder to Toland, and he had to ask his questions. What makes you think you can get away with the next one?"

She picked up the gun and pointed it at the top of my head.

"I've got no choice, Marty. You know that."

She looked at me for several seconds, then, gun still in her right hand, slid her left down to her dress, lifted it and pulled her stocking down to the knee. It fell in an uneven loop around the calf of her leg and she didn't touch it again.

"Until tonight, Marty, I wasn't sure whether or not you had talked Sandy into telling you what she had read. I was hoping desperately that you hadn't been successful, but when you said you'd see us all again it was pretty obvious."

I shut my eyes. It had worked beautifully, my little plan. All but the last part. All but the ending where I'd march someone up to Widdle at gun point and make my speech. But a steel handle slammed against my skull had changed everything, made my bluff earlier in the evening a monstrous joke at which I couldn't laugh.

"Marty, what did you think of Cronk?"

I caught my lip between my teeth, then hedged with, "I haven't changed my mind about him since the first."

"You were right on the button," she agreed. Her left hand went to the back of her hennaed hair and brought it up over her head, then rumpled it into a disheveled mess across her right ear. "A phoney doctor. How much would he get for that, Marty? A year or two, probably, and it wasn't too serious, but he was scared to death the sheriff would stick him with this murder charge. I had hoped so." She looked at me again, then went on. "And Pilcher. Imagine all that money—your dollars and mine, Marty, that he raked in on phoney war contracts. What did you think when Sandy told you about that, Marty?"

I risked a vague, "Dipping into federal funds. And Engle had the goods on him. A nice shakedown, I thought."

"A very nice shakedown, but Pilcher could afford to pay All of his was tax free, remember. It makes a difference, Marty." She brought her left shoe back against the toe of her right foot and a high-heeled slipper tumbled off to one side. She bent to the stocking, her eyes still full on my face, and made a gaping tear in the filmy nylon near the ankle and when she slowly straightened, her fingernails dug into the bare skin of her knee and thigh, raking parallel red marks halfway up her leg.

That's when I began to get the pitch. My throat tightened. Any minute now. Any minute she would point the gun more carefully and pull the trigger. There wasn't any doubt about the future she planned for Bowman. Only one of us to tell the story. Just Elsa—and the body of the killer who had almost included her in his bag of victims. I forced my lips to move.

"And the mess on the page for Elsa Doyle? That was straight too?" I asked.

"What else? And it would have been the end of my career in films. One year on a call girl list. In New Orleans, six years ago, but someone peddled it to George Engle. Someone must have seen me and recognized me, even with the red hair, and there it was. Engle was around my neck like rope. 'I must expect to get a little more money from you, my dear,' he would say. 'After all, your business is so uncertain.' And in the end he took more than I could pay. I had to stop him, Marty, and I did."

Time was running out—I had to do something, but how do you fight a girl? You're beaten before you start, damned if you do and damned if you don't. If I could distract her and get the gun away she'd still yell rape and murder.

All at once I relaxed, as I realized that no gag would be good enough to get me out of this. I was going to have to stop at least one bullet from Fred's gun. No more if I could help it, but the irony of being shot for a tussle in the hay that I didn't even get was bitter medicine. I watched the redhead carefully and when she hunched her shoulders and ripped the neckline of her dress I worked my right leg up under me, dug bare toes into the sod, yelled and lunged all at the same time, going up on hands and feet as I covered the first part of the four yards separating us, flattening out as I reached her. The blast of the .38 filled the night and a searing pain streaked along my back. My shoulders hit her shins and I felt her falling over me. I twisted back to grab the gun hand before she leveled for a second shot.

They build these Hollywood babes well. Lots of regular exercise to maintain her figure was partly responsible for her coordination, I suppose, but some lessons in man-handling she must have learned in a rougher school. She came to her feet like a bobcat, bit me on the wrist that was holding her shooting hand, scratched and kicked all at once. I managed to snag her other wrist, twisted her arm behind her, brought her hard up against me and held her there.

"Easy, Red," I panted. "Let's relax and ride with the punch. It's all over now—we'll have the smiling face of Widdle among us any moment and it won't help to struggle any more." She gave me the heel again, the hard leather scraping along my bare shin and sliding off my ankle-bone on the side. She applied her bridgework to my arm in a new spot but I managed to hold fast and when the flashlight beams began to bounce along the flagstone path she suddenly stopped writhing.

"Marty," she said quickly, "we can get together on this. You've read the evidence but you don't have to re-member it all. Don't mention my part—we can pin it on Pilcher and he deserves it. You know he deserves it—"

"Forget it baby," I said firmly, and tightened my grip against a new outburst. But she stood perfectly still, her eyes staring into the distance, and when Widdle came into sight she let out a scream for help. Holding her tightly, I waited while Bob Widdle steamed up, stopped for a quick look, then let his mouth drop open.

Before he could make any decisions I said, "Get the gun out of her hand, man. Don't do anything until you've

got all the guns in sight under your wing. Then we'll
break up this little love scene—but get that gun."

He gulped a time or two, put out a cautious hand,
and fastened on to the business end of the .38. She let
it go without a struggle.

"What the hell goes on, Bowman?" he wanted to know.
I took a breath but the redhead beat me to it.

"What does it look like?" she stormed. "An attack!
Bowman killed George and Sandy and he almost added me
to the list. If you hadn't come in time, Mr. Widdle, he
might have been successful."

"The gun," I pointed out, "was in your hand."

Widdle held up a nervous hand. "Don't say any more.
We'll let Toland handle this, and he'll probably be here
any minute. You can keep still while we wait."

I explored a little and found my wound. I wouldn't be
sitting down for a while with any comfort, but I'd live.
I looked at Elsa, then along the path where Kate and the
others were running toward us. When they came up I
heard a noise a little to one side and Sheriff Toland came
through the bushes and into the clearing. He wore field
boots and a hunting jacket and there were binoculars
slung around his neck. He stood for several seconds, his
eyes going from one to the other of us, and then Elsa
broke the silence.

"Sheriff, I'm certainly glad you came. I've never been
so scared in my life and—"

I stood and listened while she piled it on. I'd been
swimming in the pool, she told him, and she had walked
past and I'd talked to her. She went on for ten minutes,
the story getting more convincing every second—how
I'd said I'd discovered some new evidence and wanted
her to see it and she went down the walk with me to
the drain valve. And how the evidence I'd discovered
turned out to be a fraud and I'd deceived her and then

tried to pull a force job. She told him I'd carried my beach towel and had a gun, and then she looked around and pointed to the towel lying on the grass.

"I had to play along with him," she said tearfully, "and he tore my dress and I felt behind me for the handle and it came off and I hit him—"

"The hard way, Sheriff," I cut in. "She reached all the way around and slugged me from behind. A little un-handy, but that's the way it must have been. Here's the lump." I bent my head to show him but Toland didn't look at me.

"Later, Bowman. We'll get her side first."

"Then his gun fell and he fell and I was awfully afraid I'd killed him, Sheriff, but I grabbed the gun and backed away. Then—"

She finished it from there on pretty much as it happened, and I opened my mouth to say something vulgar but Toland spoke first.

"Uh-huh. Now weren't you just a mite worried, miss, while you were walking down the path with Bowman here? My orders, you'll remember, were to stay out in plain sight. By the pool where you started to talk to Bowman. How about that?"

"But he said there was something here that would tell us who had killed George and—"

"You should have stayed by the pool. You said that's where you and Bowman met, didn't you?"

"Yes, but—" She stopped as Toland turned away from her. He looked at me long and steadily, and then shook his head.

"Son, I've been out in the brush most of the evening just waiting for you to jump. Had it figured you'd strike off across the hills before long and then I'd collar you, which is why I told Bob to needle you some. But it looks like I'll have to turn you loose. There's plenty I didn't see but the light by that pool is pretty good, and unless I'm ready for a white cane this girl wasn't anywhere near the plunge tonight."

"Well, fairly close at one time," I corrected. "You'll find a cigarette lighter on the bottom. She tossed it there, as she did my silver dollar two nights ago." Then I brought the sheriff up to date on the last hour and what I'd found and how things were. When I finished I gingerly touched the red soaking through my swimming trunks and asked if we could get a patch someplace.

Toland poked his flashlight behind me for a closer look, then grinned at me. "A crease, son. You'll be sleeping on your tummy for a while and maybe eat a few meals standing up, but that's about all. We're taking the girl in with us; you can come along and we'll drop you by Doc Crandy's."

I looked from him to Kate Weston, saw her turn away, and then I followed the sheriff toward the house.

Twenty

It was Friday morning again, just a week since I'd answered my phone and heard Boreland Gregory's voice and now I was back on the beach. A patch of white bandage taped to my fanny ruled out a dip in the surf, so I had to settle for sunshine, but somehow I couldn't get comfortable. I squirmed and tried one side and then the other and about eleven o'clock I began to realize that nothing was going to be all right again until I took care of a little business still hanging fire—something about the dossier Fred had piled up on a blonde named Weston —a manila folder with half a dozen typed pages of data and it had done a lot toward jolting Marty Bowman out of the rut. I went up to the beach cottage, cleaned up and climbed into my coupe.

Riding higher than usual by the thickness of a pillow tucked gingerly under my bottom, I cruised down the boulevard and swung off at Vine, then parked and climbed the stairs for a chat with Gregory. He handed me a fat check which I tore up and then we had words. Lawsuit was mentioned, and publicity and hiring a man without credentials just to bring in an unearned fee, and at one time someone even shook a fist under someone else's nose, and in the end I left with a much bigger check made out to another name. Then I rolled on down the boulevard again.

WESTON'S, the sign said, and it wasn't the biggest place on the street but it was as nice as you'll find anywhere. On the inside you didn't see the floorspace packed with racks and cheap signs and there weren't any giggling salesgirls standing in the aisles. A trim woman in a dark dress came across the plush carpet and greeted me with the sincere warmth of a good hostess.

"May I help you, sir?"

"Yes, thanks, I'd like to see Miss Weston." We went toward an office in the rear and when the door closed behind me Kate Weston looked up from her desk.

"Marty! I—how are you—your—"

"It's almost healed." I grinned, then tossed the check on her desk blotter. "Gregory sent this along. He thought that in the light of certain developments he'd like to refund your money."

"Gregory said that?" She asked it evenly, her eyes on my face instead of the money. "What developments are these?"

"Put it this way," I hedged. "He'll feel better not keeping your money. Much better." Then I had the uncomfortable feeling she was trying to stare me down.

I looked around the room at the classy office tastefully

done in Philippine mahogony, the thick carpets, the modernistic desk. The silence dragged on.

"Kate, I've been a horse's neck," I said finally. "All those times I kept needling you about being a little Miss Moneybags and having a rich family dump the world in your lap and—but when I got home there was this file that Fred had gotten together on you. It was all there, Kate. Your going through university on some kind of scholarship and how you burned the midnight oil studying books on business and merchandising and all that. He even had a picture of the store you started in a few years ago, that little place you had first and how you were a success and the bank was willing to stand behind you on this one. It opened my eyes, Kate. I've been too busy envying other guys who've worked ahead and telling myself that opportunity is dead and you need a rich uncle to help you along." By now I was sweating a little, but I blundered along. "Well, I got to seeing it a little different, lately. I'm going up to the inn at Death Valley and work the season and save my dough. Not much, maybe, but all I can and then I'll go to a bank and there's my rich uncle named Sam who will underwrite part of my investment on a G.I. loan. I'm building that pool, Kate. Not in Beverly Hills—yet. I'll start with one out where the ground is cheaper—where they even have more need of a pool. I'll learn the business as I go, then I maybe later—"

"I could help you, Marty." She had come around the desk and I felt the nearness of her, the clean, scrubbed smell of her long blonde hair. "Not with money, or with running the pool, but in the business end. I've learned a few things about that. I'd really like to help."

"Well, sure, if you want to. We—" And then I stopped talking and she was tight against me and I had my arms around her. It was warm and sweet and wonderful. The door behind us opened and someone said "Miss Wes—"

and stopped and the door closed very softly again and
Kate hadn't even heard. When we finally broke it up I
still kept her hand in mine and looked into her soft blue
eyes.

"Baby," I said smiling, "we've got a lot of catching up
to do. We could start with lunch someplace, if you can
get away, and—"

"You can buy me a sandwich at the drugstore," she
laughed. "I'm a busy woman and you're saving for that
pool, remember?" She took her hand out of mine and
went back to her desk long enough to put away a few
papers, then turned to look at me again. "Marty, you
didn't really think I might have done it, did you? Kill
anyone, I mean?"

I looked away and fumbled for cigarettes. "No, not
really, I guess, but there were those shoes."

"Shoes, Marty?"

"Not important now," I said carelessly, "but that
night I stayed—well, there were your pumps under the
bed, Kate, and they were wet—had been out just before
I came in to see you. And you said you'd been in the
room all evening. You told the sheriff the same thing, and
I knew it couldn't be true, so—" I let it trail off, watched
her open a closet, choose a hat from the half dozen
arrayed there, and adjust it in the mirror on the wall.
When she turned around again I caught a light pink creeping into her face.

"I had a late date with a guy," she said, and looked
away. "The darn lummox didn't show up and I—well,
I went outside a few times to sort of look around and see
if he'd come back and—but I couldn't tell you that. A
girl can't appear too eager, after all, and then when I
didn't tell you, I had to stick to my story, so I gave it to
Toland the same way." She didn't say any more because
I put my arms around her again and pressed her to me
and held her close. Words weren't necessary for the next

little while and when I kissed her again and let her go the hat needed straightening once more.

Out on the street, I swung open the door of my coupe and Kate made some laughing crack about the pillow on my side of the seat and I laughed too, then fired up all six cylinders and pulled out into the traffic. It was the same car I'd driven up in but there was a difference in it somehow. Like someone had changed the windshield and all of the windows, because no matter which way I looked the world had a very rosy glow indeed.

THE END

AN OUTSTANDING SAGA OF ADVENTURE AND ROMANCE

The GOLDEN BLADE

by John Clou

"One of the most exciting stories of recent years..."   *Houston Chronicle*

"Fascinating...lusty..."   *Miami News*

"Excellent!"   *Los Angeles Herald-Express*

"Utterly enchanting adventure....pure enjoyment!"   *Pasadena Independent*

"Able, soundly researched..." *N. Y. Times*

In this thrilling historical novel, the barbarians of Genghis Khan war for girls and golden cities. Emperors intrigue while their concubines preen and plot. And out of the west rides a stranger whose sword shakes the world!

35¢

AVAILABLE AT NEWSSTANDS AND WHEREVER BOOKS ARE SOLD